THE SMUGGLER OF RESCHEN PASS

A RESCHEN VALLEY NOVELLA

Chrystyna Lucyk-Berger

Chrystyna Lucyk-Berger / Inktreks

Dornbirn, Austria

www.inktreks.com

Book cover designed by Ursula Hechenberger-Schwärzler (ursulahechenberger.com)

Cover model: Manfred Berger

Cover photos by Eberhard Grossgasteiger from Pexels and Ursula Hechenberger-Schwärzler

The Smuggler of Reschen Pass: A Reschen Valley Novella / Chrystyna Lucyk-Berger. – 3rd ed.

ISBN: 978-3-903748-25-5

ASIN: B07TJLT3R7

CONTENTS

PART I

1905–1912

1

BEST BROTHERS

1905

On my thirteenth birthday, I refused to get out of bed. The Herr Doktor was going to announce what he had in store for my future and, if it was to send me to the priesthood, as my brothers had warned me the night before, the last thing I wanted was to get up and face the judge and jury of my fate.

I looked out the window. My room was in the tower, and I had a view of Reschen Lake. Beyond, the valley's hamlets and villages spread southwards to the horizon. Our house was on a hill on the northern shore. The Schlössl—little castle—had been in the Hanny family for over a century. My great-great-grandfather, Johannes Hanny, whose portrait hung above the fireplace in the Great Hall, had been a Tyrolean landlord and of all the farms on Hanny only a few had been bought up fair and square.

My father, Maximilian Hanny, was one of two doctors in the Reschen Valley. After studying medicine, he returned from Vienna to set up his practice and marry my mother, Elisabeth. Her family ran the Post Inn in the next village. They were not as well-to-do as the Hannys, but my father had always fought for what he wanted, namely my mother. It was this knowledge that fueled the hope that, if there was still a thread of romance left in the Herr Doktor, it would be susceptible to my pleading.

I knelt before the window and watched a horse and V-cart pass by on the road above the lake. Someone crossed below in the garden. Max Junior, my best brother, dressed in knickerbockers and the stiff-collared shirt he was forced to wear on special occasions. Our dog was with him. He tossed the dog a ball. I tapped on the window, and Max Junior twisted around and lifted his head. If there was anyone I could count on to get me out of this predicament, it was him. I opened the window, the early morning cool and damp in the mid-September air.

"What are you doing?" Max Junior asked in a loud whisper.

"Are they all downstairs?"

He glanced towards what had to be the garden door. "Get down here." He smiled broadly. "You're such a ninny."

"Max, I don't want to go to the priesthood." I liked girls, I wanted to add, but I knew the teasing that would lead to. He was not taking me seriously as it was.

"Get down here, Fritzl. I promise you, it won't be so bad. Father Wilhelm's already waiting for you."

I slammed the window shut. The fact that my brother was not devastated about my eminent departure hurt me so much that I threw myself back on the bed, pulled the covers over myself, and sobbed. Life was just not fair for the youngest boy in a family.

A few minutes later, a knock rapped on my door. I stiffened beneath the duvet.

"Fritz!" It was my mother. "What in heaven's name are you still doing beneath the covers? Get yourself dressed and get downstairs. Your breakfast is waiting."

No birthday congratulations. No kiss on the forehead. My mother could hardly wait until I was out the door for good. The Herr Doktor had even gotten to her.

I sat up and swiped at the tears from my face.

"What is wrong with you?" She crossed the room and sat

down on the edge of my bed. She placed a hand on my forehead. Fever was the most feared symptom in any household. "You haven't taken ill, have you? I'll call your father up."

"Don't do that," I cried.

"What in the good Lord's name has got you all in a bother?"

"Mother," I pleaded, "please don't let Father send me away. I promise I'll be good!"

She dropped her hand. "You're not going far, Fritz. It's only Graun for goodness sake. Now get up and pack your things."

Already at the wardrobe, she opened it and pulled out the traveling case. She removed my outfit—one just like Max's—and draped it on the bed for me.

It was bewildering. My classmates—almost all the youngest in their families—were sent to the seminary over the pass. Perhaps my parents had convinced Father Wilhelm to tutor me himself. The parish house was in Graun and only a twenty-minute walk from Reschen. "But why do I have to live with Father Wilhelm?"

Mother turned, frowning. "Why in heaven's name should you have to live with Father Wilhelm?"

"To become a priest!"

"Jesus-Mary!" Mother made the sign of the cross. "You boys. Truly, Fritz, why do you believe everything your brothers tell you? I told Max Junior to… I thought coming from him… Oh, never mind! Fritz, you're not going to the priesthood—you're going to your grandparents' inn."

I sat up straight, my misery on hold. "But I thought Max Junior was going to the inn."

Impatiently, my mother began filling the case. "Both of you are. Your grandparents need extra hands, and I—with this house and your father's practice—cannot simply go to Graun every day to help them. It will be up to you and Max Junior. Your grandparents are getting on, and the Herr Doktor and I have decided it's best to send both of you."

This was an entirely different story. I was going to learn a vocation and be out from under my father's roof. What an adventure!

I was out of bed and dressed in a flash. I hugged my mother tightly and thanked her over and over. She peeled me off, scolding me for wrinkling her dress.

Leaving me to pack, my mother smiled before closing the door. I hurried, spirits lifted but still stinging from how Frederick and Max Junior had robbed me of my sleep. I decided there was only one way to get them back. I sneaked into the Herr Doktor's room, opened the wardrobe, and found his military uniform. We were never allowed in his room, much less in his wardrobe. But I knew he had what I needed to exact my revenge.

I finally found the gorget in a box, carefully wrapped, a hint of sweat stains on the edges. I imagined my father in the Prussian war, marching in the heat. I had to wrap the gorget around my neck twice for it to fit. Next, I found a black morning coat and slipped it on.

Somberly, I descended the stairs and crept to the dining hall doorway, careful to avoid the parts of the floor that creaked. Max Junior, with the dog at his feet, was cutting the top off his egg, and Frederick, as usual, had his nose in a book. My mother was not there and by my brothers' relaxed countenances, I assumed she had not scolded them for their prank yet. My father sat at the head of the long table, buttering a bun.

I gingerly placed the case on the floor and announced myself, hands folded before me like Father Wilhelm did in his services, the gorget tight around my neck. "Good morning, Herr Doktor. I am prepared to do my duty."

Max Junior and Frederick looked up, certainly anticipating finishing off their big joke, and their stunned faces shot a thrill through me. When my father raised his head, his eyes grew large as he took in my costume. My mother entered, almost stumbling into me, and gasped.

"Bless you, child." I moved my right hand in the benediction.

"What are you—" she and my father both pronounced in unison.

"I'm ready to go to God."

My father rose from his chair. "You certainly are," he barked.

He stopped short when Frederick and Max Junior broke into peals of laughter, howling and slapping the top of the table. Frederick nearly fell out of his chair as it rocked back and Max Junior shrieked, "Oh, Fritzl! You got us good!"

The chaos was what saved me. My father could not punish all three of us at once. I left the Schlössl to learn how to run an inn, and I left with my hide intact.

There were five of us Hanny children. Frederick, the eldest, trod in my father's footsteps and went to university in Vienna, with plans to practice with the Herr Doktor. He was considered nearly perfect. After Frederick, Matthias was born and Matthias quickly showed he had no interest in studies, agriculture, or any sort of purposeful work, for that matter. Certainly nothing the Herr Doktor planned for him. He finished his schooling at fifteen and set off to do what he wanted—nobody knew what that was. A year later, his body was found beneath a pier in Hamburg. He had been knifed in the heart with not a clue left behind as to what the argument or its resulting murder might have been about.

I did not remember him much. I had been too young when all of that happened. Yet, any time the Herr Doktor overheated with anger, he had a tendency to slip and call me *Matthias*. Whether by accident or to hone a point, I could not say, but it did jab my soul. I also very much suspected this was the reason my parents were pairing me up with Max Junior. It was not spoken aloud but I knew they intended for my best brother to keep an eye on me. Little did they know that the two of us were often in cahoots.

Lisl—or Elisabeth, as she was christened—was the sister born to the life every woman had in the Reschen Valley: find a good husband, get married, bear children, survive those burdens for as long as the good Lord saw fit. At sixteen, my mother and the Herr Doktor introduced her to Georg Roeschen in Graun, a well-read man from a family of merchants. Lisl was married off without a word or whimper. Though I saw her on the occasions when our paths had opportunity to cross, I could not say that at my age I knew anything intimate about her life after marriage. We were born eight years apart, and that was practically a generation. Georg was a good enough soul. Quiet, reserved, a dedicated Catholic, mayor of Graun, and head of the local rifle guild. Lisl was better dressed than most, well respected, and bore Georg three boys. They took occasional shopping trips to Meran and—like the Habsburgs—visited the baths and took long walks around the city, returning with a variety of new cures and oils and other exotic wares.

Max Junior was born next, and I came into the world not twelve months later. He called me Fritzl and was the only one to do so. Together, we were known as *best brothers*. We were inseparable, and the entire valley was wary of our pranks and our ability to throw caution to the wind. We tested the boundaries of our formidable Herr Doktor. In return, he made sure our mother accompanied us to Father Wilhelm every Saturday afternoon to confess our sins. And I reckoned the reason we attended the earliest Mass next day was to get Max Junior and I to Communion before we could sin once more.

As we grew older, it became clear that our parents had been wholly misled to believe that learning the hospitality industry would lead Max Junior and me to salvation. The Post Inn, from the first day, was a playground for our chicanery, the borders of which were limitless.

2

—————

THE TIES THAT BIND

1905–1908

Max Junior and I discovered early on that, though the inn would eventually be our inheritance, we had absolutely no authority. That belonged to two women our grandparents employed. Anna Winkler was a sour-mouthed matron with a husband prone to violence. He'd broken a glass or two and many a tooth or fist in our inn. The second one was Jutta Mair, a feisty, dark-haired lass with a widow's peak, high cheekbones, and a sharp tongue. She was quick as a whip. The two women were fixtures in that inn, so Max Junior and I had no choice but to obey their orders. It was Jutta we respected more than Old Anna. Once, when she grated my nerves, I asked Jutta who'd made her the boss. She put her hands on her hips, the dish towel she held flicking like a cat's tail. The defiant stare wilted me right on the spot.

As Max Junior and I grew older, the inn was the focus of quite a few renovations, and we did all we could to help out. We were developing a reputation not for just being hard workers but also as generous entertainers. We were also made to handle a few of the rowdier guests, which was nothing to sneeze at. Most of the time it was our own folk who were the worst when they'd had too much drink. They came repenting the next day and mostly to Jutta.

I recognized that, more often than not, the men from the valley came to the inn to be served by her. They eyed her, teased her, and provoked her to snap a dish towel or flick their hats off their heads when they were too bold. There was always a lot of laughter, and a few times I suspected Jutta of stepping around with one or the other.

Since she was responsible for cleaning all the rooms, Jutta had a key ring attached to the sash around her waist. We could hear her coming except when she was sneaking up on Max Junior or me to catch us at something. But she never reported us to our grandparents.

Later, as we grew older, Max Junior and I stayed up with Jutta long after closing and played *Watten*, drank wine, and gabbed until the morning. Afterwards, we'd all crawl up the stairs to the attic floor, where Max Junior and I shared a room and where Jutta was located down the hall. Things started to change for me when I began having dreams about her. Next day, I stayed out of her way, mortified by the stains I'd found on my bedclothes in the morning.

When Max Junior and I finished school, my father had a mind to send us to Innsbruck to university, but my mother eyed the both of us and asserted herself, saying it would be wasted time.

"First of all, you can't send them both to the same city," she said. "Secondly, you can't separate the two." My mother turned to my father and gave him a single determined nod. "They're good at the inn. They've been practically running it all this time."

And that decision was made to my grandparents' great relief. They vacated the inn's apartment on the ground floor and moved into a cottage outside of town.

Though our grandfather continued to oversee the business,

Max Junior and I stayed in Graun to run the Post Inn. It was a decent living, and yet I still longed to make my own mark. A dark shadow stretched over me and caused me great unease, for I knew it was the ghost of Matthias—or the residue of that which he'd left behind.

3

______

TOBACCO

1911

I was working the bar one night when the local boys came in with someone new. Marius Egger, from Nauders—just north of the pass—had a round face with cheeks that looked as if they'd been placed on as an afterthought. His nose was bulbous, and his eyes set deep in his head. He compensated for his looks with a brisk humor and a talent for entertaining. He made everyone laugh. I was quick to join in when that was the case. Between Marius and me, nobody could escape the pranks I dreamt up. We became quick friends.

He visited us regularly. On one such occasion, I was behind the bar refilling beers when Marius called me over. He was sitting at a table with our local boys, everyone gabbing and drinking and joking. When I came, he made space for me on the bench, and Max Junior, who sat next to him, slid over as well.

Marius leaned in, effectively shutting out the rest of the group with his bulk and suddenly very earnest. "I've been watching you two all this time," he started. "You ever consider getting into the cigarette business?"

Max Junior and I looked at one another but said nothing.

"I got good tobacco coming in from Egypt. It would give our Tyrolean plantations a run for their money."

Max Junior rose and jerked his head towards the door of the *Stube*. Marius and I followed him into our apartment, where my brother indicated the table against the window. When we were seated, Marius reported that paper cigarettes were growing in popularity, especially amongst the working class. The problem was that all tobacco products were controlled by the state monopoly—the Imperial-Royal *Tabakregie* –and we'd be running smuggled goods from the plantation in Memphis.

Goose pimples rose on my arm. Something exciting was about to happen. Heart pounding, I took my cues from Max Junior, who was looking pretty sober about the idea. Getting into tobacco smuggling would be lucrative, but striking up a business with someone you hardly knew—a scheme—required sense and careful consideration. I was absolutely convinced that there was good money to be had in tobacco, in good tobacco. And cigarettes, well, the working class was a massive market.

Max Junior and Marius were already negotiating a detailed plan, and I tried to think of something wise to say, something that indicated I knew what I was doing.

"How do you know the people?" I asked. "Who are they?"

"Family," Marius said, appraising me. "My uncle runs the plantation in Egypt. My cousins just returned from Memphis. They've been planning this for some time."

I gestured between Max Junior and myself. "And why us?" To my relief, my brother did not show any displeasure about my butting in. "What's in it for us?"

Marius jerked his head at the door. "You're the next post stop. Easy enough to coordinate deliveries to the south. Besides, your family's got reach."

"He wanted to know what's in it for us," Max Junior said, and I tossed him a grateful glance.

"Seventy-thirty."

Seventy! Then I realized he meant we'd get thirty.

"Fifty-fifty," Max Junior and I said together, and we shared a look of mutual understanding.

Marius laughed and shook his head. "I love first-timers." He leaned in, still grinning. "Sixty-five–thirty-five. It's my best offer."

"Sixty-forty and we can shake on it," I said. I savored the rush to my head. "If we get caught, it will be severe."

Marius stuck out his hand to me first, not Max Junior, and I smiled back but he pulled his hand away before I could shake it. "Sixty-five, thirty-five. Take it or regret it."

Max Junior stuck his hand in Marius' and heat crept up the back of my neck. Afterwards, Marius pumped my hand up and down and Max Junior went and unlocked the cabinet near the door. He removed a bottle of schnapps and poured each of us a thimble, and toasted our new venture.

Later, we ironed out the details. Marius would take the northern territories from Nauders to Innsbruck. Max Junior and I would take everything from the Reschen Pass to the south. We would all sell tax-free rolled cigarettes directly to the guesthouses and inns.

Once a month, I travelled up to Nauders to coordinate with Marius. The cigarettes took off, just as Marius had predicted. I oversaw the sales and deliveries from Graun to Meran, then farther to Bozen and finally to Trent. Hardly a single guesthouse said no, and when they did, it was the women who forbade it. It made no difference. Max Junior and I were soon making a nice living from our cut. We were able to install one of the first gas stoves in the valley and, a little later, indoor plumbing. This was followed by an ice cellar, the only one for miles around. We were careful to spread these upgrades out, careful not to cause too much suspicion and get the controllers to check the books. The folks in the valley were astounded by our business acumen. Max Junior and I were making real names for ourselves.

A few weeks before the Lenten season, I was in Nauders when

I heard how controllers had caught one of our runners. He'd tried to escape and had been shot. In memoriam, Marius and I shared a few drinks. When I wanted to head for home, a winter storm had crept in on us, snow falling thick as ash in a raging forest fire.

Marius set up a room for me. Next morning, I awoke with a heavy head to a bright-blue winter sky. There was half a meter of fresh snow everywhere. Marius insisted we take the skis and hike around the road, and then I would ski back into the valley over Graun's Head. I said he was insane. Our heads were splitting from the drinking the night before. He said he wanted to check out a new route. We trudged through a blinding snowscape lit up by the sun and powder.

Before the climb, there was a small homestead ahead of us. A dot of a person was shoveling to the stable. It wasn't until we were just above the farm that I saw it was a woman. She stopped to watch us pass but, when I paused on the trail, she got back to furiously shoveling.

"We should help her out," I said. "Probably wants to get to the animals."

To my surprise, Marius held me back. I chided him for his laziness but he shook his head. "You want nothing to do with that there."

I scowled at him. "What, her? She can't do anything to me."

He started to protest, but I turned my skis towards the stable yard.

Behind me, Marius shouted, "I'm not going down there."

"Morning," I called to the girl. I unbuckled my skis. "Need some help?"

The sun was behind her back and blinding me, sending sharp stabs through my aching head. Her silhouette stood stock still as I approached. I had the idea I was prowling on a frightened wild kitten.

"I'm Fritz," I offered. "From Reschen. Visiting my friend over there." I pointed Marius out, and true to his word, he was still standing at the top of the path, leaning on his poles. As soon as he saw me looking his way, he lifted them in a flabbergasted gesture.

"Mind if I help?" I asked her again.

Once I was under the shade of the house, I could finally look at her without the sun glaring in my eyes.

She was the most beautiful creature I'd seen in my entire life. A genuine enchanted wood sprite. The first thing I did was curse Marius. The scoundrel had tried to deter me from what must have been Nauders' best-kept secret.

4

CECILIA

This was a girl I would have done anything for. I was in the presence of one of the gentlest, sweetest, most tender lasses I'd ever seen. Her golden hair fell about her shoulders. Blue eyes, the color of cornflowers, were framed by white-blond eyclashes. I was trying not to drown in that field of cornflowers. She had fair skin and a delicate nose with gracefully sculpted nostrils. I didn't ask again whether I could help her. I would have moved mountains for her. I gestured for the shovel, and she handed it to me as if she had stolen it and was giving it up. I paused long enough to see a blush of shyness bloom over her cheeks, and my heart turned to putty.

I shoveled to the stable door. It did not take me but a few minutes, but in that time, I made the decision to come back for her.

When I leaned the shovel against the wall, I could barely look at her, so much did it hurt.

"What's your name?" I asked.

Her eyes skittered about.

I made a coaxing sound, and her gaze landed on me, held steady. It took my breath away.

"Cecilia," she whispered.

"Fritz. Fritz Hanny. From Reschen." I left it at that. I was nervous, and Marius was shouting for me to come.

I hiked back up and turned to see her one more time but she was gone. Had I imagined her?

"Who is that?" I asked Marius.

"Leave it be. She can't be more than fourteen years old."

His unwillingness to discuss her kept me mum about my plans for her.

I made an excuse to go back to Nauders within the week. This time, the snow was melting from the constant *Föhn*, and it was dangerous to ski on. *Firnschnee* was what I had—snow that melted into corn-sized balls, froze overnight, and was treacherous as it slowly melted again. But hiking to Nauders would not bring me past Cecilia's farm, so I skied.

In the valley, the snow was almost gone, leaving rivulets streaming down the dirt road and pooling in the ditches. Something told me not to venture down the drive. I waited to see whether anyone would come out. When the door to the shed next to the stable opened, a stocky man stepped out—cap askew —with dark hair plastered against his brow. He did not even glance my way. Behind him came the girl. Cecilia. Unlike the man, she spotted me. Even from where I was standing at the top of the drive, I saw her shoulders fall back before she hurried after the man and disappeared into the house.

Something told me to keep walking, but I lingered at the top of the ridge, making it seem as if I were adjusting my skis. She came out a few minutes later, carrying a basket, and tossed feed to the chickens. She glanced up at me, then jerked her head as if to say, "Go on."

To the right of the house was a field with a hay shed and a deep creek cutting through it. I pointed in that direction and headed down the road. Where nobody could notice except

Cecilia, I cut through the field, and when I reached the shed, I waited behind it because there was nothing else I would have been rather doing.

And she came. Like a mouse. And when she turned the corner to find me, she looked surprised.

"Cecilia, you're very brave," I said. "I'm glad to see you."

She looked down at her faded brown clogs.

"Who is that man at the farm?" I was afraid of the answer.

She gazed at me with those stunning blue eyes. "Papa," she whispered. "I can't be here. I have to go back to the house."

I was terrified she would bolt, so I grabbed her hand, and she jerked back with a small cry. I held on tighter.

"I'm sorry," I said and released the pressure just enough to assure her I meant to eventually let go.

She stilled, the way animals did when they decided it was better to do so.

"I won't hurt you, Cecilia. I'm not here to hurt you. Please."

"I have to go." It was a plea and something about it made me want to hang on harder.

"Can I come again? Please let me come again," I begged.

She shook her head at first, stared at my hand grasping hers. I let go and it dropped to her side. When she nodded, just the slightest twitch of a yes, my heart flipped.

Cecilia was not the forbidden fruit in the Garden of Eden. Our valley and mountain lives were anything but a paradise. No, Cecilia *was* the Garden of Eden, and now that I had found it, I did not want to leave. Her father might have guarded the gate, but I would find a way to break in.

"I'll be here tomorrow." I would spend the night at Marius's. "Where can I meet you?"

Hesitating, she turned and pointed in the direction of the woods along the field.

"There. Wait for me there. Papa sleeps after his midday meal.

I'll come then." Then she dashed around the side of the hut and ran back to the house.

Tomorrow. It could not come soon enough.

❖

I watched her coming through the field, and I was reminded of rabbits being hunted. She stood still, half facing the woods, one side of her face tilted back towards the house. After a moment, she continued in my direction.

She was shy when she found me. I was prepared. A moss-covered path led through the forest, gnarled roots and shrubs catching on the hem of her skirt. I told her about the inn and how Max Junior and I owned it, though we really did not yet. We would though. I told her about the Herr Doktor and how Frederick would take over the practice, and she looked at me askance.

"You look like you don't believe me," I said.

"I do. Of course I do. It's just that… Well, your family… It's quite well to-do." With the little hope that shined through her uncertainty, I knew Cecilia would be mine. She did not pull back when I took her hand this time. Her palm was cool, and I put it to my lips, sinking into that field of cornflower blue. I drew her in a little closer and, when she resisted, I whispered again how she should not fear me.

At the same time, a thought slid into my mind. *Oh, but she does,* it whispered.

"I would never do anything to dishonor her!" We both startled at the vehemence in my tone and when Cecilia stared wide-eyed at me, tugging from my embrace, I dropped my voice to a hoarse whisper. "You," I said. "I meant you. I'd never dishonor you."

I let her go, defeated. She turned sideways and looked as if she were measuring the distance between us and the farm. What had gotten into me? "Cecilia?"

She turned back to me but did not look up. "You're scaring me."

"No," I whispered, pained. "I'm sorry. I just… I was just taken by you." Then, hopefully, "You smell like flowers and milk."

Just the slightest smile.

I tipped my head and tried to get her to meet my look, to see that I was smiling, too.

Her eyes darted to mine then finally rested on them. Her lips parted. "That's nice. That's the nicest—"

"Would you meet me again, tomorrow?"

Again, measuring. This time, me. She nodded and then was gone.

The second day, it was easier to coax Cecilia out of the house and into the woods with me. We were more relaxed with one another. Though Marius was impatient and wanted me back home selling his tobacco, I could not leave. On the fourth day, dizzy with anticipation, I told her my plans.

"I will marry you, Cecilia." I turned her hand upwards and kissed the inside of her wrist. I could feel her pulse racing beneath my lips, as if her blood had just freed itself. I felt a rush of extreme satisfaction. She made a startled sound in the back of her throat, and I could not—even if I had wanted to—stop. I moved my lips up her arm, then placed her hand around my waist and pulled her in. She stiffened against me, and I lifted her chin.

"May I kiss you, Cecilia?"

She shook her head, and I had to step away.

"Why not? Do you have a beau?"

Again, she shook her head.

"Am I not good enough for you?" I swallowed hard to keep my temper under control.

"That's…not it," she stuttered. "My…my father…"

I spun her back to the path and pulled her in the direction of the farm.

"I'll speak to your father," I shouted over my shoulder. "There is nothing he can do against our wanting to be together."

Cecilia protested, trying to yank her hand out of mine, but I held on. I only stopped when she called my name over and over, panic rising in her voice.

"Fritz! Fritz! Don't do it," she panted. "He'll kill you."

"I own an inn, Cecilia." I faced her. I was also making a small fortune with my dealings with Marius. Money could buy anything, especially—by the looks of him—Cecilia's father. "He should be grateful to marry you off to someone like me! From a family like mine! What other choices are there, Cecilia? Huh?"

Her lips trembled. I grabbed her by the waist and kissed her, felt her sweet mouth on mine, and flicked my tongue over it. She moaned and pulled, but I held her close and kissed her once more.

Any longer and I would no longer be responsible for my undoing. I released her. "It's settled then. I am not leaving Nauders until you are my bride."

When we stepped out of the woods and walked across the field, I did not listen to Cecilia's protests. In the barnyard, her father was outside, shoeing a scrawny horse with patches of sores on its rump. When he looked up, I saw the red-rimmed eyes, the drawn face, the meanness and the disgust that seemed to make him larger as he stared at us coming down the drive. I steeled myself for a fight. Cecilia had been right. This was not going to be easy, but I had a good many advantages. If I could start the discussion, I was certain it would go in my favor.

"Fritz Hanny, sir," I said, stretching out my hand.

He'd stood up by that time and was twisting the horseshoe hammer in his grip as if he was considering striking it over my head. He did not take my offered hand. Instead, he looked askance and spit. I dropped my arm to my side.

"I told you to stay in the house."

He was addressing Cecilia and I moved to block her from him. He cocked his head, eyeing me up and down.

"What is this?" He sneered at me. "Rutting season and you sniffing around my girl? He do something to you?"

Cecilia whimpered, shook her head.

"Sir, I have no intention of dishonoring your daughter."

"Dishonoring my daughter," he said slowly. "Dishonoring. Very fancy talk for a fancy pretty boy." He took a step at me. "Boo!"

I flinched but stood my ground. "I'm Fritz Hanny, sir. Dr Hanny's son. Of Reschen."

He raised his brows in mock surprise. "The party boy? The one claiming he owns his grandparents' inn? I know you're running with the Egger fellow. Cecilia, you come to me right here. Now!"

Cecilia slinked over to him, disappearing behind him like a shadow.

Her father raised his fist at me but did not strike. "Who do you think you are, Fritz Hanny? She's just a girl! My girl."

He came at me so quickly, I was slammed straight onto my back. The impact took the wind out of me. I watched from the ground as he stalked over to the freshly shoveled manure pile, took a bucket, and scooped it full. I started to scramble away but had barely made it onto all fours before the bucket came down over my head and a kick landed right between my legs. I yelped in pain, manure tumbling down my hair and shoulders.

"Horseshit, that's what you are. Now get off my land before I have a mind to make you into fertilizer. Get!"

I fled. I fled over the field, avoided the town and fled over the pass. Only then did I stop only to clean myself off in a creek. As I stared at my stained face on the water's surface, I vowed I would find a way to get back to Cecilia. I'd find a way to get rid of her father. How dare he? He, talking to me as if I were the last scum on earth!

Max Junior would help me. And Marius. And with that, I realized that it was *Fasnacht,* the Tuesday before Lent. Max Junior would make me pay for leaving him alone at the inn the entire carnival weekend.

5

FASNACHT

MARCH 1911

In the inn's yard, beneath the apple tree, Max Junior was cutting up old branches. He dropped the saw and stalked over to me when he saw me coming.

"Where the devil have you been?" He leaned towards me and sniffed. "Is that shit? Are you covered in shit?"

"I'll tell you about it later. I need to rest." He was so sour, and I was still aching.

But my brother would not let it go. He followed me into the inn, yelling at how irresponsible I was, and did I not know that Shrove Monday was the busiest night at the inn and tonight we had to prepare for the parade?

At my room, I slammed the door in his face and threw myself onto the bed, pillows over my head. Max Junior finally stopped pounding on the door, and I fell into a deep sleep. When I awoke, it was to the noises in the *Stube* across the hall. It was time to get ready for the parade.

I washed up and went into the dining room. It was filled with the boys from the local rifle guild. Max Junior set down his costume and came over to me.

"Where the hell have you been, Fritzl? Some of the boys said you're chasing a gal in Nauders. What the devil are you thinking?"

How the hell did anyone know about Cecilia? "It's none of their business and none of yours."

Max Junior frowned. "Damn it, Fritzl. She really got to you. What'd she do, spurn you? Why else would she dunk you in cow shit?"

Laughter and jeers from the boys at the bar. My fist swung on its own, and connected with Max Junior's chin. His head snapped back. He reeled into a table and staggered. Wide-eyed, he grasped his jaw and moved it back and forth. I was just about to ask if I had broken it when he charged me. I tumbled into the boys, who hooted and hollered. I wrenched myself away from my brother, but he swung fast, knocking me in the ribs. Someone had me by the shoulders and I shook myself free, spun around and was prepared to pound their face when I realized it was Jutta, arms now spread out between my brother and me.

"What is wrong with you?" my brother shouted at me.

"Boys!" Jutta shoved Max Junior away.

"No, I want to know what the hell is wrong with Fritzl!"

I was sorry for having taken my frustration out on him, but he deserved it. "I told you. Just leave me alone."

"You're a sore loser," Max Junior complained. "It's no wonder that Nauders girl doesn't want you."

I made to go after him, but Max Junior's friends held me back.

"Stop provoking him," Jutta shouted. "Now, I'm pouring you two a schnapps, and then I want you to be best brothers again."

It took half the bottle before I felt able to get into costume. Everyone else was ready to proceed. We were dressed as demons, all of us. Our wooden masks were grotesquely carved with wide eyes and sharp teeth set in grimaces, and the tops were adorned with cow horns. We wore fur-covered tunics and capes. Klaus

Blech, our leader, wore a wolf's pelt on his head, which trailed all the way to the ground. We had bells and chains tied to our wrists and ankles. It was time to scare winter to hell.

The parade started at the Post Inn and would go all the way into Reschen, ending at the Schlössl, where our parents' garden was set up for the festivities. It was something our family did each year. An important occasion not just to celebrate the coming of spring but to also catch up with the locals, discuss politics, to gossip and—most importantly—to scout out available girls. Our animalistic ritual of pairing up.

That put a real damper on my mood. I pined for Cecilia, irritated with myself for not fighting back. I was convinced that if her father came across me now, I could kill him with my bare hands. At the thought, my anger boiled just beneath the skin. I was itching for a fight again. A proper one. With blood. One that I could win.

We lit our torches and assembled in the churchyard, a wide circle of demon-masked men. The music started. The beating of drums, the clanging of cymbals, the rattling of our bells and chains. It was a cacophony of noise. There were jeers and laughter as we made our way along the parade route. Children screamed, some hiding behind their mother's skirts. Others—goaded by their friends—hooted and hollered at us, darting out, daring each other to touch something of our costumes.

We demons, in the meantime, marched, turning our heads this way and that. I'd stuck a flask into my breeches and now pulled it out and tipped the bottle to my lips beneath the mask. I had only two small eyeholes, and even with the torches, I could see little. The shapes of people ran into one another, blurred. I tried to see where I was, but I could not tell how far we had come. Was I near the sundry goods shop? Or near the bank?

I veered towards the crowd and people scattered. I saw another demon and recognized Max Junior's voice. He was making animal noises and waving his bell-clad arms. Two girls ran screaming from him. A few men jostled next to one another. They reminded me of nervous sheep.

"Kidnap," my brother called.

Our ritual included grabbing someone, throwing them over our shoulders to carry them away. More often than not, the demons targeted a woman.

Scanning the crowd through my small eyeholes, I landed on Frederick. He was standing with a young woman from Reschen. Frederick's sweetheart? I felt a lump in my gut rising. Max Junior made to go after a young fellow, but I tapped him on the shoulder. I jerked my masked head towards our brother, and Max turned his demon face on him. I heard Frederick laugh nervously, and he protested, stepping between us and the girl. Fine. Let Frederick be our victim.

I rushed in behind Max Junior and bent down to grab Frederick's feet. Someone shoved me from behind, and the force made me tumble, and I bowled Frederick over like a skittles pin. There were cries of pain. It was Frederick, but it was also me. I had caught myself with my hands, and my wrists hurt where they'd taken the brunt of the fall. My palms were scraped up. Stinging, I rose on unsteady feet. Frederick was still on the ground, Max Junior trying to help him up. People were laughing and trying to help Frederick. Someone else asked if he was all right.

"You idiots," Frederick moaned.

"Wasn't me who knocked you over." Max Junior's voice was muffled behind the heavy mask. "Your stupid younger brother, that's who that was."

Frederick was upright again, and I made as if to grab him, but he slapped my arms away. "Stop, Fritz. You never know when to stop!"

I cackled and waved wildly. "Such a baby," I taunted. "The poor Herr Doktor junior."

"I'm hurt." Frederick was holding his elbow. The girl—Margit —was trying to help him. Max Junior had already moved away, intent on an older child.

"Come now," I teased Margit. "I got scraped up too. Come over here and tend to a man. My brother's a ninny."

Frederick shoved me away. "That's enough, Fritz. I mean it."

"Leave him alone," someone behind me said. A woman.

I swung my head in her direction. Through the small holes in my mask, I saw full breasts beneath a tunic, and hands on hips. I looked up at the face, but already knew she was Jutta. Meddling Jutta. She would do.

I had my arms around her waist before she could open her mouth again. I heaved her over my shoulder. The cry of surprise sent a satisfactory thrill through me. I growled and shouted, the bells around my legs and arms jangling. She was like a sack of grain. I wrapped my arms around her knees, and she screamed and laughed at the same time.

"Fritz, put me down. Put me down, I say."

"Who's Fritz?" I asked.

"You, you idiot. Put me down!"

Idiot? I wrapped my arms tighter on her knees and swung around in circles, the crowd scattering out of the way. I pretended to let go, just relieving enough pressure to give her the feeling that she would go flying over people's heads. Her hiccupped laughter turned into cries of real fear.

I nearly lost my balance, and Jutta became hysterical. I grabbed hold of her again and swung back into the street. I was far behind the rest of the parading demons. My breathing was heavy. I could still smell manure somewhere on me. I was thirsty. It was hot as Hades beneath the heavy costume.

"Put me down, Fritz," Jutta cried breathlessly. "That's enough."

Sweat ran into my eyes, and I shook my head. Beneath the mask there was no relief. Jutta began slipping off my backside, and I grabbed her upper thighs and hitched her over my shoulder more securely. She was going to get herself hurt like this.

"You're mine," I growled. "Stop fighting me."

"You're going too far, Fritz!"

"Am I?" How far was too far?

We were just crossing between the town lines of Graun and Reschen. Here, the crowd had thinned down to practically nothing as the parade-goers were headed to the Schlössl. Jutta was uselessly beating her fists on my heavy fur vest. I swung her around again.

"Fritz, you are the biggest, meanest bully. I swear. Put me down. And you stink!" Her tone had changed.

I pictured Cecilia. Her father. How he had me all wrong. The humiliation. And now Jutta had to rub it in. She was crossing the line.

Between the storehouse and the blacksmiths was a narrow alleyway that led down to Reschen Lake. I veered off into it, dizzy. I needed to take the mask off. I needed a drink. I had to put Jutta down.

I sidled in and Jutta cried out.

"You're scraping me up!"

Just before the alleyway opened onto the path, I slammed her onto her feet, then leaned up against the wall of the storehouse and ripped off the mask, dropping the pelt cape from my shoulders.

"You are such an ass!" Jutta was crying. "You hurt my head."

"Stop your whining."

She shoved me, but I was already leaning so heavily that the rough stones jutted into my tunic. Her hair was a mess, all undone. She sniffed, more angry than in pain, I guessed. She liked being in control. Now I had it.

"Did I scare you?" I jeered. I reached into my breeches, and Jutta put her hands on her waist. "What?" I laughed. I removed my flask. "Here, have a drink."

She punched at my shoulders and swung at me one more time, but I ducked out of her way.

"Stop your hysterics, Jutta. You're going to spill the schnapps. Come on. Take a swig."

"No!"

"Have a drink. It's all just fun and games. You know this is the way things are done."

"Not if you're hurting us," she protested.

She finally took the flask from me, and I heard her gulp.

"Have another," I said, weary. "I'm already drunk."

I wiped the sweat off my brow and watched her take another swig. The cool air was helping to set my breathing back to normal. We still had a ten-minute walk to the Schlössl.

"What's wrong with you today, Fritz?" Jutta demanded. Even in the dark, I could tell she was eyeing me critically.

"I was just beginning to forget, and now you have to bring it back up?"

"Oh, Fritz. This girl has really set you in a mood. Just get over it. I hear she's the prettiest thing in Nauders, but she's just a child. What's she going to do with a big, tall bully like you?"

Good for nothing. Party boy. Idiot. Bully. In a haze, I pushed myself from the wall, reached out, and grabbed her by the shoulders. She whimpered, and I squeezed harder, digging my nails into her skin. I could taste blood coming from my lip.

"Nobody talks about Cecilia that way. Especially you."

I yanked her closer, and her breath caught. I stared down at her face, just making out the contours, the high cheekbones. Something stirred in me, and I shook her again. When I tried to kiss her, she turned her face away, and my mouth fell on her hair. I grabbed her chin and yanked her face up to mine.

"Just one kiss," I said. "For old times' sake."

"We never—"

I spun her up against the wall of the storeroom. I knew those stones dug into her back. Her whimpering and struggling was just making it all worse.

"Be still, woman! I just want a stupid kiss. Come on. I'm all wound up. Just a kiss and we'll go to the party."

I pushed up against her, my whole body on hers, and the stirring in me so strong, I squirmed in it.

"The devil take you," she hissed.

"Be careful," I whispered into her ear. "Remember who you're talking to."

The bells on my wrists jangled as I fumbled at her breasts. She'd been teasing me for years with those breasts. They were full, and soft, and ripe for the picking. I bent my head and pulled the collar of her tunic down as far as it would go. I licked the exposed skin and tasted sweat.

"Fritz," she gasped. "Please. No."

I remembered the feel of Cecilia in the woods, the pulsing of her wrist against my lips, her sweet look, her big eyes, wide and pleading. Her mouth finally on mine. I moaned her name. A fog crept in on me and I fought it. To hold onto the image of Cecilia. The sensations. I could not let it take those from me.

Beneath me, things had finally stilled. Just the occasional hitch of breath. I yanked her to the ground. She tried to twist away and I wrenched her onto her knees. To beat the haze that would soon swallow me up, I freed myself from my breeches with one hand and hitched up the dress with the other. This was how far. This.

The bells jangled, keeping me awake. Just once. This.

The flesh was damp, cool. Warmth. I wanted warmth. I pushed and sought. The bells. This. I sank. *This, Cecilia.*

The bells fell silent.

Deep through the fog, ragged and wet breathing. Not mine. On the cold, hard ground, my body shook uncontrollably. My throat, dry. I knew then.

"Jutta?"

There was no answer. The only sound was of fabric rustling

and stifled sobbing. I could not place where she was, for my entire body was spinning round and round on the ground. I said her name again. No answer.

"This didn't happen," I called out. "You hear me? It didn't happen."

6

———

JUTTA

JUNE 1911

"I need you to go back up to Nauders," Max Junior said. I was standing at the reception desk, and he leaned opposite me. "You haven't been in almost three months, and I need you to go."

I looked up from the card deck I'd been shuffling. "You go."

"I have been. Every time. It's your turn. Get over that girl already, would you?"

Behind me, the kitchen door opened. Rattling keychain. Jutta. Max Junior greeted her, and she muttered something in return. Out of the corner of my eye, I saw her balancing a cup of coffee on the way to the post office. I only looked up when the door closed behind her.

"What's with the two of you anyway?" Max Junior said.

"Nothing. I've been telling you for months. I don't know what's crawled into her drawers."

Max Junior moved away. "Tomorrow. Nauders. We need the cigarettes." He went into the kitchen.

I sighed and slammed the card deck onto the table and began calculating the balances due on the rooms. The door to the post office opened again and Jutta stalked over. She

34

dropped a stack of letters on top of my book. They looked in order.

"Next time, sort the mail yourself," she said. "It's past nine. People are coming to pick up their post. It's not my job."

I lifted the envelopes and flicked through them. Nothing interesting. What had I expected? A letter from Cecilia? I glanced at Jutta going up the stairs to the rooms above. Her back was stiff, her hand sliding along the banister.

I was trapped. I'd have to go to Nauders tomorrow. The idea of running into Cecilia made my stomach lurch. There was no way I could face her now.

The night after the events in the alley, I'd awoken in my bed, sore and sorrowful, and I had no idea how I had managed to get back home. The church believed the priest taking our confession was a nonjudgmental representative of God and capable of absolving all sin. All I believed was that Father Wilhelm was the assigned keeper of the entire valley's secrets. Confessing would mean voicing, and voicing would make it true. Jutta's stony silence, her rigid back, the dark shade her eyes had taken on, all of it led me to believe she had come to the same conclusion. It was our secret, not to be told. And still, the secret was so big I did not know how I could face Cecilia. She would surely know as soon as she lay eyes on me.

I slammed the guest book shut and went to do duty at the post office. First person to come in was Georg, my brother-in-law.

"Morning, Mayor," I said.

"Morning, Fritz. I'm expecting a few things."

I rifled through the separated post. A letter stamped from Munich had his name on it.

"Here you go. The Geological Society?"

Georg eyed the envelope. "Well, let's have a look, shall we?"

We'd just learned about the reservoir the Imperial engineers were proposing. Something about raising Graun Lake to connect with Reschen and harness the Etsch River's power to make electricity. I was excited by the prospect, but there were others who were up in arms, including my brother. By the way Georg was frowning as he read, I guessed there was more trouble brewing. And I was right.

That afternoon, the dining room was full. Max Junior and I called the men at the *Stammtisch*—the table for regulars—the mayor's advisors. There was Herr Prieth, the baker. Young Martin Noggler, the blacksmith. Anton Federspiel, the banker. Klaus Blech and his father, the local butchers. Father Wilhelm sat in as spiritual advisor, representative of the church and its agendas. My father was also there, of course, and Frederick too. My eldest brother was the most recent addition to the circle. Max Junior and I sat nearby, listening in on the arguments for and against the reservoir.

Martin Noggler scratched his fiery-red hair. "I don't know, Mayor. Our property goes right up to the edge there, and if they raise the lakes, I lose land. Do I drop my irons and pick up a fishing pole now?"

Georg placed a hand on the blacksmith's forearm. "We'll do what we can, Martin. Of course I will suggest replacement land."

Georg explained scientists were coming to conduct ground tests to check the feasibility. I guessed that was what the letter had been about.

"So it's not certain yet?" Frederick asked.

The Herr Doktor shrugged.

"Then we wait until we find out what they have to say," Frederick said. An obvious assertion of his young wisdom.

"What about this inn?" Martin Noggler gestured into the otherwise empty dining room.

"And the church," Father Wilhelm added. "Surely all the buildings anywhere near Graun Lake will be affected."

Just then the boys from Arlund walked in. Hans and Hugo Glockner, twins the size of northern giants, ran their parents' sheep farm. Whereas Hans was quiet and kept to himself, Hugo was the outgoing one. He and I had spent a night or two up until dawn carousing and having fun. They both greeted Max Junior and me and took a seat at the *Stammtisch*.

With them had come the Thaler boys, Johi and Jonas. Their farm was one of the most prosperous in the valley, and the family was well respected. The boys were known for being reliable, hard working, and faithful to God and country. Irritating.

Johi approached Max Junior's and my table first, dark hair swept back from his brow, smelling of sheep soap and clean sun-dried clothes.

"*Griaß-enk.* You seen Jutta?"

Just the mention of her name sent shivers through me. "I imagine she's upstairs cleaning rooms."

He sighed. The fellow was depressed. About a week after the carnival, I had seen Johi and Jutta beside the chicken house. He had looked desperate, and I could tell from the way he had been wringing his hat that he was pleading with her, begging for something. But Jutta had grown that stiff back. Her head was turned away, and I had the impression that if she looked Johi in the face, she would burn up.

Max Junior had come up to me where I watched at the window.

"Heavy hearts," he'd said.

"What do you mean?" I kept my eyes on the two.

"They've been walking together for a few weeks. Johi's always been sweet on her. Last time you were in Nauders, he was testing around Hugo like you would around a sinkhole. Wasn't he still interested in her? Would it be okay? That kind of thing. Hugo just laughed, said Johi didn't need his permission to go chasing after the hardest catch in the valley." Max Junior had chuckled, in that way that indicated he knew everything. He did not.

"Our Jutta," he said, "is a confounding woman. Suddenly she's got cold feet or something. I swear, she's got a heart of stone. I feel sorry for Johi."

I had turned away from the door. Whatever chance Johi might have had, it was over.

From then on, any time he was down in Graun, Johi hung around the inn, his hope for some sign of affection or a change of heart all fluffed up around him. And every time Jutta made sure to veer out of his way, a little more of Johi seemed to shed off and float to the ground.

The mayor and his advisors were still talking, and Johi seemed uncertain whether to sit with them or with us. He shifted from one leg to the other, then sank into a chair at our table. As soon as he did, Jutta walked into the dining room and Johi sprang up like he'd just been stung by a hornet. His face changed from anxiety to hope to disappointment all in a single second.

Jutta halted, obviously not expecting to find him there, but her eyes flitted over him, as if that, too, would cause physical pain. They landed on me, and her expression went blank. She turned stiffly to the *Stammtisch*.

"Herr Doktor," she called to my father. "I heard you were here. May I have a word with you?"

My heart hammered in my chest. This was it. Jutta was going to give this words. Because she'd had to sort out the post today? Or was it because Johi was here now?

My father was examining her from afar. "Are you ill, child?"

Jutta's chest rose as she took in a breath. "Something like that."

Her eyes grazed me again as she turned to leave. My father, paying us no mind, pressed his hat on his head and left the dining room. By the sound of the next door opening and shutting, he must have gone into Max Junior's and my apartment.

Johi sat back down. "You think she's all right?"

"How should I know?" I grumbled.

Max Junior rose, clearing up the table. "Come on. The lunch guests will be coming soon."

Johi glanced over his shoulder at the door again.

I wanted to smack him across the head. Instead, I said, "You may as well give up."

He raised sorrowful eyes. "She say something?"

I shrugged. "I think she's got other things on her mind is all I'm saying."

When the door opened to the dining room again, it was the Herr Doktor. He had me square in his sights, and the expression on his face scared me stiff.

"Get in here!" He jerked an arm into the hallway.

Across the way, the apartment door stood open and I could see Jutta hugging herself, pacing back and forth.

This was it. I was done.

7

———

SWEETS

1912

Jutta's baby came late. My father met us after the delivery. He examined the newborn's short neck, the extra skin around it, the flat face and nose, and pronounced our son a mongoloid. My father had not had to say anything, though he did. Without words, he once again made sure to let me know I'd failed him, embarrassed the family name. Aloud, he urged us to send the child to an institution. That argument led to the end of any amiable exchanges I had with my wife. Jutta protected that infant like a dragon, silently—like my father—blamed me for everything.

I had long before come to the conclusion that I would atone for my sins for the rest of my life. And Jutta? She was being punished for bribing my father. *Violated* was the word my father used when he referred to what I had done to her. *Violated* is what she had done to me when she spilled our secret the way she had.

When my father relayed Jutta's story to me, the walls had begun to fall around me. On the tip of my tongue had sat the only thing I had left to fight with, and as soon as I opened my mouth, it rolled off and spilled into the room, stopping Jutta in the midst of her pacing.

"How do we know it's not Johi Thaler's? She was walking with him not so long ago. Look how she avoids him now. It could be his."

Jutta had shot daggers at me with her eyes. There were dark circles around them.

"I'll go to the constable," she said. "This is a waste of time."

My father immediately raised his protests, tried to calm her down. This just would not do, he said. Anything she wanted, he would give her. Money. A special doctor. Whatever she wanted.

"I want this all gone," she had wailed. "I want you to take the last three months away. Can you do that, Herr Doktor?"

My father made noises. I understood nothing, as if I were under water. It was just noise, noise, noise. My thoughts turned to Nauders, to Cecilia. I could not be forced to care about Jutta's problems, with Cecilia just over the pass.

At some point it was the stillness that pulled me back into the room. Jutta was sitting on my grandmother's couch, her head in her hands.

"Anything, *Fräulein* Mair," my father said. His tone was formal, stiff. "Just say it and I will see to it."

It had not required any of my imagination to understand what kind of discussion they had been having up to that point.

After a long silence, Jutta scanned the room. "This inn. I want this inn."

"What in heaven's for?" I cried.

By the revelation that grew on her face, I could tell it had not been a premeditated idea. She was earnest, and the wheels were turning in her head as we spoke.

"I've never had anything of my own."

"Well," my father said. "We're certainly not just going to hand the inn over to you."

"No, of course not." She indicated me impatiently. "But if Fritz and I get married."

"Father," I started, "she's six years older than I am."

He whirled on me with vehemence. "You should have thought about that before you pulled your peter out." His eyes bored holes through me with the disgust he held there. "You're rotten, Fritz. Just like—"

"Like Matthias," I jeered. "Yes, just like Matthias!"

He rolled his shoulders back. To Jutta, he said, "You're about two and half months along." He glanced my way and seemed to be considering something, conceding to me. As if that was the apology I might need. "And you're sure it's Fritz's?"

Jutta held my look, emotion rippling over her face like on a lake's surface in a breeze. She finally turned away.

"He's not my first, Herr Doktor. That you have guessed correctly. But Fritz is the only man who has..." Her hand fluttered to her throat, and she held it as if she had to squeeze the words out. "He's the only one who has... In the last four months," she whispered.

My father's anger had almost been tangible. "We'll need to marry you right away. Avoid the scandal. As for the inn, I cannot just give it to you. The boys—Max Junior and Fritz—will own it rightfully."

"Fine," Jutta said. "Then I own one-third."

I scoffed. "We can't just take what she wants from Max Junior. What if he gets married and his wife wants a third too? We're just going to give any woman who wants it a third of the inn?"

My father scowled at me. "Mathematically, that would not work. And Max Junior keeps his half. It's you who will be reduced to nothing now."

A joke. My father had made a joke at my expense.

Jutta rose. "I want nothing of the inn until both boys die. Then it's mine. And no matter what happens, I have a place to stay if I so choose."

The Herr Doktor narrowed his eyes. "What should happen? What are you referring to young lady?"

Jutta threw her hands into the air. "How should I know? Or

does someone here understand God's plan better than I?" She faced me, and I saw the first glimpse of genuine hate. "Look at him. If he's not out to kill himself like Matthias did, then I don't know what! What do you call this? This life you're living, Fritz?"

Six months after my entrapment, I was on my way to Nauders. I played and replayed the events that had led me impossibly far from Cecilia. And in six months, there had been no sign of her. I never asked Marius about her. I didn't want to know. More than anything, I did not want Cecilia finding out what had become of me.

The winter had been rather mild of late, and when I went to Marius's place, his first question was about Alois.

"How was the boy's first Christmas?"

"He's fine. He grows stronger every day."

Marius did not yet know of Alois's condition. I could not bear to share it.

"He'll be big and strong like his papa," Marius said and laughed. "As long as he's not an idiot like you, he'll be fine."

I had to turn away or strike him.

Marius packed up my rucksack with cigarettes, and when I took it from him, the load was noticeably lighter than usual.

"What's the story?"

"Conflicts on the Mediterranean coast."

I sighed. "I've been thinking, Marius. What if we approached the manufacturers in Borgo Sacco? Make a deal with them for distribution? Their cigarettes are very popular and still cheap."

Marius gnawed on a toothpick. "You have a connection? Someone you can talk to?"

I nodded, thinking of a man who had turned our cigarettes down because his cousin ran the plant in Borgo Sacco. Though he already received a good supply from his relative, he had always been good to Max Junior and me when we came by. Visiting him would also give me an opportunity to get away from the inn. From Jutta.

"I'll let you know, Marius. Give me a couple of weeks." I patted the bag. "Whatever we do, we need a new supply line."

Marius nodded, eyes half-closed, assessing me. "Yeah. Do that. I would be mighty grateful to you if we could find another way."

I left him, and went to the sundry shop in Nauders for the things we needed at the inn. The one in Graun would close before I got back. I walked in on a few women doing their shopping. The owner of the store was cutting fabric from a bolt of cloth, and his wife was measuring sugar onto the scales. I stood behind one woman and waited my turn.

When the bell that hung on the front door rang again and again, the customers turned and dipped their heads in greeting. I did not, but when I heard the response from one of them—that sweet voice!—I whirled around and faced Cecilia.

Except it wasn't Cecilia. Not the Cecilia of my memories. Certainly she had the same cornflower-blue eyes, the same delicate nose, but this Cecilia was scrawny, her hair frizzed at the ends, and she held a snot-nosed toddler in her arms. Her breath caught when she saw me, and she wilted even more than she already was. This Cecilia was downtrodden, ragged. I saw her catch her lip between her teeth, saw the pink tip of her tongue lick her lips before she gazed back up at me. She hitched the baby higher into her arms.

"Hello, Fritz."

I touched my cap. "Cecilia."

"How have you been?"

Better than you, I wanted to say. Or maybe not. "I've been—"

"Sir?" It was the sugar woman. "How can I help you today?"

I stammered at first, looked over my shoulder, afraid Cecilia would run away. I wanted her to. And more desperately, I wanted her to stay. I gave the shopkeeper my list. It was extensive enough to buy me some time with Cecilia.

I moved to the edge of the U-shaped counter and beckoned her to follow me. She did.

"You have a child."

Cecilia's eyes widened. "Oh, no. It's not mine. I mean, it is, but it's in my charge. I'm…I'm married now."

I raised an eyebrow. "To whom?"

"Eberhardt Müller. His wife…" Cecilia halted. "She passed away. And my father…" She had tears in her eyes.

I bent over her. "Are you all right, Cecilia?"

The child started fussing. Cecilia patted its back and sniffed.

"I couldn't stay with my father, Fritz. And you…" She raised her eyes to me. "You never came back for me."

Her words punched a hole through my gut. She had been waiting! What had I done? It took all I had to ask whether this Eberhardt Müller treated her well.

Her eyes searched my face. "He is an older man. Patience is not his virtue."

I understood and had to hold myself back from taking her into my arms.

"He has six children. And all he wants is a seventh from me, but I…" Her voice faltered once more.

She was a child herself! I had to lean on the counter. "Cecilia—"

"Please don't think poorly of me."

"Me? Think poorly of you? How could I?" Weren't we both imprisoned by our circumstances?

She grabbed hold of my arm and turned so that the baby was out of my sight. She whispered, desperate. "If you say so, I'll leave with you right now. If you would have me, take me with you. Wherever you want. I would follow you to the end of the world." The first tear escaped. "You are the best man I ever met, Fritz."

But how I was not! "I'm not who you think I am."

She took a step towards me, backed me into the counter. "But you are. I have to believe that. Please, Fritz. You promised me."

The baby grabbed a fistful of her hair, and she smacked the hand away. The child cried out and pouted in my direction. Accusation was written on both of their faces.

"I've done nothing right by you, Cecilia. I haven't been..." *true to you.* "You would be worse off with me, I tell you. I swear in God's name."

"Don't say that," she begged.

"Your father was right. I'm not good for anything."

"Young man!" The shopkeeper waved me over to the register. "Your packages are ready."

I looked above Cecilia's head at the other customers in the shop, certain they were trying to listen in. In a firm tone, I said loudly, "Madam, it was good to see you. I congratulate you on your new family."

Cecilia stared as I pushed past her. I heard her wail, or it might have been the toddler.

"Is there anything else you need?" The shopkeeper eyed me.

On the counter in front of me, a jar of hard candies in all the colors of the rainbow. The yellow ones, golden like Cecilia had once been. "Yes. I'll have seven lemon sweets."

She picked them out and wrapped them in brown paper.

Just before I passed Cecilia, I took her hand like I had on our walks. I held it for a moment—felt its warmth—before pressing the packet of spun sugar into her hand.

"One for each child," I said and hurried out the door.

PART II

1914–1920

8

WAR

1914

My grandfather's funeral was on July 24. Too young to understand death, all Alois wanted was to see his uncle Max and me parade with our rifles with the Imperial-Royal rifle guild. But when Jutta found me showing him the weapons, she declared war on me.

Angry with how she had lost her temper over nothing, I left the inn early and joined the other *Standschützen* in the churchyard. Max Junior and I had transferred to Company Three of the Nauders battalion since we were no longer registered residents of Reschen. From the age of seventeen, we reported to the shooting range at least four times a year. Recently, we were all attending the range weekly. After the assassination of our archduke, conflict was in the air, and we riflemen were preparing to defend ourselves against the Russians should the call come.

The bells of the church tolled, and we filed in, then lined up in the first pews for the service. My brother and I each carried the colors of Graun. I glanced at Max Junior as Father Wilhelm took his position above my grandfather's coffin.

A week before our grandfather had died, Max Junior and I

had been out at the range. In passing and as we aimed at our targets, Max Junior had said, "Opa's ready to go."

"To war?" I had been astounded. It was all we ever talked about. And Opa had been a respected old marksman, but he had also been over eighty.

"No," Max Junior replied. He dropped another bullet into the chamber, then raised the rifle. He took the shot, hitting the target square on before looking over at me. "He's ready to die."

Our grandfather passed in his sleep just a few days later. After our grandmother's death the year before, he had steadily grown disinterested in everything around him. I'd never have calculated that old man for being sentimental. But still waters ran deep and all that.

Father Wilhelm started the Lord's Prayer, and we all stood. As we took Communion and I watched Jutta pass by with Alois, I thought how the two of us would never pine after the other. On the contrary, I believed she wished me dead. No matter how much I tried, she was never happy. Each time I went to her bed, it was a double-edged sword I lay down with. On the one hand, she was the only woman I could satisfy my urges with, and the only way to do so was to remind her of her duties to her husband. I tried to imagine I was with someone else—Cecilia, more often than not. Sometimes a fine young woman stayed at the guesthouse, and I would think of her in the rooms above.

After a night like that, I usually drank more. And when I drank, I said things I did not really mean. I knew damned well that I was digging my own grave as a father and a husband. How I should do it differently, I did not know. Jutta provoked me.

Father Wilhelm gave the final blessing, then motioned to us *Standschützen*. We rose and followed the coffin out from the church to the cemetery. I winked at Alois, who grinned back before Jutta stepped between us. I watched as he hobbled on thick legs, his ankles twisting grotesquely. At three, he was still as unsteady as an hour-old colt.

Father Wilhelm blessed the casket, and my mother lay the Graun colors on the coffin. We raised our rifles to the air and pronounced the three-gun salute the old man deserved. I heard Alois, high pitched and excited. When we were finished, the funeral party dispelled to the Post Inn.

Most people sat with their families, but I stopped at the table with the Glockner boys, Hugo and Hans already hunched over their bowls. I was tall too, but these two were giants, and their matching beards made them look more like bears than men.

"Don't mind if I do, boys," I said in greeting.

My sister, Lisl, approached with a pot of soup. "Fritz, the family's got a seat at the table for you."

Hans and Hugo looked up at the same time, as if they shared the same neck.

"Nah, I'll keep them company." I smiled up at my sister. "Jutta's had enough of me for one day. Started in on me this morning."

"What did you do now?"

The Glockner boys dropped their heads in unison and went back to slurping their soup.

"What do I know, Lisl? Doesn't matter what I do—it's always wrong."

She smirked. "Knowing you, she probably had every right."

I sighed and lifted my spoon. "Should've known better than to expect any sympathy from a woman."

When she'd left the table, I turned to Hugo. "Weren't you once sweet on my wife?"

He blinked back at me.

I shook my head. "You can count yourself lucky, is all I wanted to say."

❖

The following Tuesday, Max Junior and I were doing some mowing up in the fields, when all the church bells started tolling. I glanced up at the sun. It was long past the early morning Mass. This was a call for assembly. One look and my brother and I swung our sickles onto our shoulders and sprinted down to the churchyard.

War. We were at war. It could not be anything else.

A good number of folk were already milling about by the time we got there, and Mayor Roeschen was rifling through official-looking papers.

Our company's second lieutenant was Klaus Blech, the butcher's son.

"What do you know?" I asked him.

He eyed Max Junior and me. "You going to war with sickles, boys?"

Max Junior grinned at me. "This is it then."

"We're mobilizing to the eastern borders," Klaus said. "The frontier in Galicia. Orders are we're to only defend her right now. The war is with Prussia, not with us." He cocked his head. "Yet."

Max Junior and I dashed off without another word. We had to get our rifles prepared, find something to carry bread in, get better clothes, and find axes, a couple of spades. By that afternoon, we would be heading north to meet with the rest of the battalion in Nauders.

Jutta stood in the doorway to our apartments as Max Junior and I helped one another fashion kits out of what we had and could find. For the first time, the woman was speechless. An hour later, Max Junior left to seek out his sweetheart—a young girl on the other side of Graun Lake. When I was ready, I bent down to Alois. It pained me each time to look at those almond-shaped eyes, the toothy grin, the stubby neck, and the stunted body of my son. This would have been a moment that I, as a father, could tell him he was the man of the house. But my son would require care for the rest of his life.

"Well." I stood before Jutta. I took her in, felt nothing but a gnawing trepidation. "You might just get your wish."

"What in God's name do you mean?"

"I might die. It's a war."

Jutta scoffed. "You're defending a border, Fritz. You're not allowed to attack."

I bristled. "It won't be long before they'll give us orders to fight."

"Then you had better take care of yourself," she said. "And Max Junior. Watch out for him."

I hesitated before reaching to kiss her, and she hesitated before letting me. Just her cheek. Neither of us could bring ourselves to kiss each other on the mouths. Not since we were married had we ever.

As I gathered my things, I felt her hand on my arm.

"Fritz," she said. "I don't want the inn that badly. Understand? Stay alive. Alois needs you."

I looked at my son. At least somebody did. And that made me only feel worse.

❖

The Glockner boys, Klaus Blech, and Jonas Thaler were just some of the fellows who were with our company. Johi Thaler stood with us, cursing himself for not being able to leave. Being the eldest son on the farm, he had not been called and was to stay in the valley. We were beholden to tradition, tied to our land. What else were we off to protect?

We met more of our friends and colleagues in Reschen as Company Two joined us on the road north. All in all, we were jovial, excited, and happy to be with good friends.

When we arrived in Nauders, we found more of our comrades, Marius amongst them. Max Junior and I pulled him aside and inquired about what would happen with the cigarettes.

Marius nodded. "I've been preparing for it. I've got a couple of trusted associates."

We heard him out, but Max Junior and I were pretty nervous about losing our business. What would be left when we returned?

Marius shrugged. "This won't last long," he said. "We'll be in and out and back at it before anyone can take over our territory."

Our companies were called to order. The battalion's commander had arrived. An older man in *Tracht* and wearing the two stars of a lieutenant on his collar called us to attention.

"I'm your commanding officer," he said. "Eberhardt Müller."

I started. Cecilia's husband! Her keeper!

He focused on me right away. "You have a problem, boy?"

I could not look away, though I knew full well I had to. He was maybe in his late forties. Cecilia was about seventeen now. Lieutenant Müller had a full beard and was built like a bull, and though he was at least two heads shorter than me, I knew he was trouble.

He stalked up to me and stared upwards. Max Junior squirmed beside me, and Eberhardt Müller's eyes shifted to him before glaring at me once more.

"We know each other, boy?"

I shook my head.

"I asked you a question! Do you have a problem with me, boy?"

I looked straight over his head.

"That's a 'No, Lieutenant' then, rifleman. We're not drinking schnapps on the shooting range! You will learn soldiering right here and now!"

"No, sir," I barked.

"What's that? Are you defying me?"

I was confused. "No, sir!"

"You want to cause trouble with me?"

"No, sir!"

I could smell him beneath me. Farmer smells. His feathered cap just reached my throat.

"What's your name, soldier?"

I swallowed. What did he know of me? "Fritz Hanny, sir!"

The feather tipped to the left. He was squinting at me. "Maximilian Hanny's son?"

"Yes, sir!"

"Well, well." He turned on his heel, and I breathed again.

To the rest of the battalion, he proclaimed, "This is war now, boys. And you will learn discipline. Your play days are over. Do you understand me?"

We all barked in the affirmative.

He marched on up and down the lines, preaching about how we were hardly recognized as troops but as patrols. That we'd be conducting drills on a regular basis because—he stopped before me again and eyed me up and down—we were going to learn discipline. Once and for all, discipline!

When it was over, we loaded up, and our journey to the eastern frontier began. It took us three hard days to reach the far side of the Galician border. We were quartered in a small village outside of Chernivtsi, in the Carpathian foothills. It did not take long for Marius, Hugo Glockner, Max Junior, and I to get to work. We charmed the villagers in a heartbeat, for in a brilliant move, Marius had packed enough cigarettes, so for the next two weeks we had one feast after another. We had *salo* and bread, the bacon fat and rinds greasing our stomachs for the bottles of vodka and *samahon* that followed. The home-brewed spirits were hellish, but when we were introduced to a honey liqueur, we learned to take down the clear spirits and leave the sweet stuff alone. The locals drank us under the tables, so to speak, as our carousing mostly took place around a bonfire. There was hardly a morning we did not wake up to heads as big—and fragile—as ripe melons.

The war was nowhere near us. The Russian border remained quiet. Besides Lieutenant Müller's orders to keep us in drills, we were relatively free to do anything we wanted. At first, we rarely saw him, but three weeks in and enough time for Marius and the others to charm the locals, our commanding officer suddenly began appearing at the nightly gatherings. By that time, most of the boys were paired up with local girls.

Marius was the mediator whenever things got heated. He had managed to win the affections of a corpulent light-haired maiden himself. Halyna was pretty and had a loud laugh, and Marius and she were like two peas in a pod. I was not interested in any of the girls, though the dark-eyed beauty in whose house Max Junior and I were assigned to seemed to have me in her sights.

As soon as Müller came to the bonfires, my mood soured. Cecilia's husband was the worst amongst us. He barely drank, but his hands were everywhere. He got hold of the dark-eyed girl, and I watched as he pulled her into his lap, his hand on her back, the other on her thighs. I bristled, thinking of Cecilia. Thinking of how he must be with her.

My smoldering must have been obvious, because Marius caught my eye and jerked his head at the lieutenant. I shook my head, my eyes burning with the desire to strangle the man. Marius patted Halyna's rump, and she stood from his lap. He rose and strode over with a bottle to me.

"It's not worth it, Fritz," he said and handed me the *samahon*.

I shook my head and raised the drink to my lips. It burned more than usual, and I choked, wishing I had a piece of bread.

I wiped my mouth with the back of my hand. "What is this horseshit?"

Marius laughed, but it was cut short when he stared across

the way at Müller. The older man was nuzzling the girl's neck, the muscles on his forearm bulging as he pressed down on her thigh.

"He's sick," I muttered.

"She's pregnant," Marius said.

"The girl?" I turned, astonished.

"No. Cecilia." Marius sighed and took a swig from the bottle. "Second one. You wouldn't recognize her, Fritz."

I groaned inside. I could not imagine it. I stood up and stumbled—drunk—to the cottage where I was staying. My body ached, and I found it hard to breathe. My Cecilia. Both of us, ruined. One way or another, I would avenge her.

9

HOMEFRONT

1914–1915

The Russians attacked in August, and we were ripped from our revelry. Orders to hold the city of Lemberg came quickly, and our companies fought in tough battles. Our lack of military training became woefully evident. What we had done on the shooting ranges of Tyrol had been child's play. And we were in danger. Our lack of respect for Müller's leadership caused our companies to quickly fall apart. We were, each of us, fighting for our own survival.

On patrol one night in a quarter near the opera house, I rolled some tobacco for myself. It was a quiet night. My rifle was propped up against the barriers, and I lit my cigarette, looking up at the night sky. Above me, on the barricade wall, was the shape of a man.

Time was suspended. *Russian! He will kill you!*

The shadow moved through the air like a large cat in the night. With a swiftness and wildness I would have never guessed I possessed, I withdrew my knife from where it hung on my belt. With the handle firmly in my hand, I aimed at anything solid again and again. Again and again.

There was no noise save for a rushing sound in my head, as if

I stood beneath a waterfall. The mechanisms my fury set off were fully automated, and my motions became like a silent chant or a prayer.

It was Hugo who wrestled me off the corpse, and when I saw the blood—so much blood!—a different noise filled my head. When I tried to stumble away, the boys all jumped on me and covered my mouth. The noise was me, screaming. Primal. Horrible. And beautiful. I was alive.

Matthias! I am alive!

I dreamt of my dead brother that night. Of his body lying on a Hamburg pier, of the pool of blood he must have left behind. I dreamt I stood over him and then he opened his eyes and laughed.

I awoke the next day to a fuzzy haze in my head, the hangover left over from a gruesome nightmare. When I crawled back to where I had been the night before, the Russian had been long removed but the bloodstains were the evidence I needed. It had happened. *Fritz, that had happened. And you're alive.* I was better than him. I was.

❖

As reserves, we received little respect. Wherever the Prussian or Imperial-Royal battalions came to replace or support us, we were made fun of and jeered at. I was sick and tired of the war, sick of the lack of sleep, the harsh conditions.

What we lacked in military training, Marius, Max Junior, Hugo Glockner, and I made up with our resourcefulness in black market tactics. We knew that Müller suspected us, was out to catch us and have us brought before a military court and hung. Half our game was to stay ahead of him.

It was a cold day in November when the four of us slithered into the city and broke into an abandoned warehouse, the neighborhood shattered from an earlier battle. Hungry, tired, and cold, we meant to pilfer what was left. Into sacks and rucksacks we stuffed what supplies we could find, including things we could later trade with. On the way back to our position, we realized something was very wrong. Our companies had packed up and moved on without us.

I dropped the sack of potatoes I was carrying and gazed at the ominous faces of my colleagues.

"We're done now, boys," I said. "They'll shoot us for desertion."

Marius shook his head. "We have to go find them. Now."

I was certain Müller had done this on purpose. Since the day we'd led a farmer's pig away and had the cook slaughter it and on a spit before Müller could make us bring it back, we were our battalion's heroes. Standing there in the middle of the dark Lemberg street, rapid shots firing all around the city, I was 100 percent certain Müller had been waiting for such an opportunity. We four had grown too popular, and he hated us for it. The feeling was mutual.

I pulled out my flask and unscrewed the top. "Only thing to do is lubricate ourselves for the long march to headquarters."

We each had a pull and lugged our loot through the streets, dodging the areas we knew were under fire. It was not easy, but we did make it to where we reported to the major, who was more than perplexed to see us and maybe a bit relieved too.

"We need all you boys," he said. "Italy's declared war on us. All the *Standschützen* are being sent to defend our borders to the south. You will receive further orders in Landeck."

In Landeck, we discovered that the riflemen were being assessed. Our men were assigned to either defend the borders to the far south or assigned to patrol and reconnaissance missions in the Chain of Alps. For months, the rifle companies throughout

Tyrol had been training every able-bodied man in preparation for what the empire already suspected: Italy would not remain neutral.

For the first time, we received something of a uniform: armbands in black and yellow. The Imperial-Royal army was afraid that the *Standschützen*, if captured, would be treated as guerillas. As for weapons, we were not supplied with anything other than what we had taken with us from home in the first place.

"May as well as have taken our sickles too," I said to Max Junior later. "Double the power."

He smirked, and we waited for our transport to take us back to the pass. We were heading home.

❖

The majority of the men from the Reschen Valley had already mobilized to the southern borders to meet Italy head to head. Of those of us returning from Galicia, two companies took positions along the Ortler range to the Reschen Pass. Another company was set up from the Reschen Pass to the Brenner Pass. When I calculated, I came up with about one man for roughly every thirty square kilometers, and no artillery.

I was assigned to patrol nearby, as were Max Junior, Hugo Glockner, and Jonas Thaler. Marius was sent to the Ortlers, where Müller was waiting for him. We all had time for a brief visit before we had to report for duty.

Back in Graun, I clapped Jonas Thaler and each of the Glockners on the shoulder before leaving the churchyard and crossing over to the inn. It was late May and it had just rained. The air was cold but fresh. I breathed it in, standing beneath the apple tree in the yard. Behind me was the church cemetery. Before me, the kitchen window, and Jutta was working on something, like kneading dough. When the back door opened and Alois waddled out, my heart sank. It had been ten months since I had left for Galicia. Where most fathers would be impressed by a son's developments, Alois had not changed at all. He was still unsteady, and he still grinned in ignorance. He had no idea what hardships awaited him.

I called to him, and he looked up as he came down the stairs. I should have waited. He stumbled and fell down the last two steps. I rushed to his side, but he was already screaming. I lifted him to brush him off and heard the door open.

Jutta came down the stairs, huffing and exclaiming. "Alois! Fritz! What in God's name?"

I stood up as she scooped the child into her arms. Her tone was both accusatory—what had I done? What had I been thinking?—and breathless with surprise.

"We're at war, now," I said.

"Yes, yes, I know." She hugged Alois closer. "Why are you here then?"

"I have less than a day before I have to report. I'm going to be stationed at Graun's Head." I hesitated. "I wanted to see you. Let you know that I am here."

Jutta lowered Alois, who had stopped crying, back onto the ground. He now grasped my leg and began nagging me about seeing my rifle. My wife brushed a hand over her hair, as if she realized in what disarray she was.

"Well," she said. "Then if you are so close, I expect you will return as often as you can."

"I'll get something to eat then. And pack something up for me. Jonas Thaler and I will be working in shifts, but I won't be making the journey every night. I'll come when I can."

"And Max Junior?"

I pointed to the west. "Over there."

She nodded. "Will he be coming too?"

"He's stationed too far away. He's seeing his girl now. She'll attend to his needs."

Jutta pressed her lips into a thin line.

I pointed to the pile of neatly stacked wood near the chicken coop and barn. "You're managing an awful lot of work, Jutta. Rest assured, I'll be here to do what needs doing."

"Fritz…" Her eyes darted over the pile.

I waited.

She seemed to reconsider. "Come inside. I'm baking now, but I have some bread you can take, and cheese and jam." She turned to go back into the house, Alois by the hand, and listing the other things she would pack for me.

I glanced back at the stack of wood. It was an awful lot that woman must have done, and I did not believe she had done it all herself. So who was helping her?

❖

A late snowstorm hit me in the shepherd's hut a week later. I pulled on a second layer of gaiters against the snow and went on patrol. The snow would melt within a few days, but I had to assume that Jonas would not be on time to relieve me with that much accumulation.

Near a ravine, I found a man's tracks—coming from the north —from what had to have been the early morning hours. I frowned. Who was here?

It was then that I realized one of Marius's contacts was surely smuggling along our old route. I followed the tracks a bit, coming to the path that led into the Reschen Valley. I let it be. It was no threat to me, except that I considered the fact that maybe it was time to get my cut on the wares again. I could wait for him to return, find out who was involved, and then pick up where we had left off. Surely I would find a way to get back to the selling and delivering. I just needed the new contact in Nauders.

Nauders. At Graun's Head, I could see into both valleys, and I thought of Cecilia. She would have had her baby. Her second one. I brooded. Müller, stationed somewhere along the lines on the Ortler range, was days away. He would not be coming back home whenever he wanted. Which meant that, if I wanted, I could just go by and check on Cecilia. See how she was doing. Whether she needed anything.

When Jonas finally arrived to relieve me, he watched me pack.

"There's someone trekking through here," I said. "Someone from the north, I assume."

The way he reacted, I paused in what I was doing. "What? You know who it is?"

He shrugged and looked guilty. "It's Johi."

"What's he doing up here? I thought he'd have been stationed with the rest of the rifle guild to the south."

"He's the eldest. Hasn't been called yet," he said.

I nodded. "He will be soon enough. So what's he doing up here?"

Jonas eyed me. "I thought you knew?"

"Knew what?"

"Marius gave him your route."

I dropped my rucksack. "Johi? Johi's been carrying the tobacco?"

Jonas nodded.

"Well," I said. "And delivering them to my inn, I suppose?" The woodpile was beginning to make sense.

Jonas looked up, cautious. "It's not what you think, Fritz. He's just helping. We could use some of the money too."

"Sure, sure." I lifted the bag and slung it over my shoulders.

"But now I'm back. And you can tell him to back off." I stepped in front of him. "From my cigarettes and my wife."

I left him with that. Let him chew on that for a while. I stared in the direction of the Reschen Valley. Jutta was the last person I wanted to see right now. I headed north.

❖

Müller's farm was located on the other side of Nauders. I passed by Cecilia's father's place, and it was looking run down, as if it too had been under fire in some battle. The man deserved it for abusing it all: his farm and his daughter.

I found the place I was looking for, asking as discreetly as I could, and it was nearly nightfall by the time I arrived. The snow had not fallen this far down, and the temperature was so warm, I had to shed a layer before continuing. When I came up to the house, there were two young boys working in the stable. I guessed them to be between eight and twelve years old. One was pitching hay. The younger one stood on a step stool, brushing down a workhorse. The place was doing pretty well in comparison to Cecilia's father's. The boys each stopped in their work and stared at me. I shifted the armband up higher and greeted them.

"Look." The boy with the horse pointed. "It's a reserve. Patrol."

The boy with the pitchfork jerked his chin at me. "What you want here?"

"A little respect would be in order," I said. "I'm the reason you're not on the Italian front yet."

He frowned. "You here about my papa?"

"No," I said. "Your mother home?" But I didn't wait for their answer, though the older one demanded to know what I would want with her.

From inside the house, I heard a baby wailing. I knocked on the door and let myself in. In the first room, a little girl—the one who had to have been the toddler I'd seen in the shop all those years ago—was playing with a doll on the floor. When she saw me, she leapt up and backed into the corner, the doll abandoned before her.

"I'm not here to hurt you. I'm looking for your mother."

I heard the baby crying again. I stepped out into the corridor once more and passed the stairs leading to the next floors, and came to the scullery. There she was.

Cecilia was stirring a pot of what must have been soup, the wailing baby in a cradle and a toddler at her feet.

"Cecilia?" I took off my cap.

Startled, she looked up, started to say something that sounded like *Eberhardt*, and stopped when she took me in. I saw recognition bloom on her face.

"Fritz," she finally breathed. "What are you…" She put a hand to her mouth. "Is Eberhardt…"

I realized what she must have been thinking. "No, no. He's fine. I'm not here to spread any bad news."

Cecilia stepped away from the pot and brushed down her stained apron. She was in a simple flaxen shift the color of dung, and her hair was a mess, but beneath all that disappointment, all that hardship, all the weariness, I saw that most beautiful girl I had ever laid eyes on. Her soft blue eyes darted towards where the baby was crying, but I wanted her to look at me. She started for the cradle, but I reached it first.

The baby stopped crying when I stood over her. Immediately, I saw she had Cecilia's same blue eyes.

"Is this your youngest then?" I remembered how she had denied the child in the shop. "Your baby this time?"

She indicated the toddler crawling at her feet. "He too."

The boy looked like Eberhardt. I had no interest in him.

I lifted the baby girl from the cradle, careful to be gentle. She was quiet now, examining me. She was Cecilia through and through. An absolutely perfect child. I pressed her to my shoulder and bounced her up and down.

"I think she likes me," I said. "What's her name?"

"Elisabeth."

I laughed. "That's my mother's name." I held the child before me. She could have been mine just as much as Eberhardt's, so much did she look like Cecilia.

Cecilia watched me, and I wanted to dispel her anxiety.

"I wanted to see how you are doing," I said. "I have about a day, a day and a half at most. I thought I could help."

Elisabeth gurgled, and I pressed her to me and kissed her cheek, so soft and delicate. I nuzzled it some more.

Cecilia's chest rose, and she glanced around the scullery. "Would you…would you like to join us for supper?"

The two boys from outside rushed in.

"What's he want?" the older boy demanded. "Is papa all right?"

Cecilia gathered herself. "He's just a friend. Of your papa's. In his battalion. He needs—"

"A place to rest," I said. I eyed Cecilia, and she was flustered again. I turned to the boys. "I'm on my way to meet your father."

"He can have the room in the attic," the older boy said.

Eberhardt had certainly told him to be the man of his house.

With Elisabeth still in my arms, I helped Cecilia take the bowls out and asked where the rest of the children were. There should have been eight altogether. There were only five here.

"The eldest, Anna, is working in Landeck at a hotel," Cecilia said. "And Eberhardt took the two older boys with him. He didn't want them going south." She looked embarrassed. "We only have the one rifle."

I nodded and could not help placing a firm hand on her

shoulder. "Don't worry, Cecilia. The army will outfit us soon. They will be fine."

She lowered her head towards my hand, and I thought she might kiss it. She stood still though, and I moved to the table. She spooned soup into our bowls, and I asked the older boy permission to lead the prayer, and we broke bread.

That evening, tucked in the drafty attic room, I waited. After dinner I had helped Cecilia clean up, and in the scullery we had brushed up against one another. Each touch sent a fire through me. I had allowed her all the pretense of putting the children to bed, of pretending I had no interest but to spend the night under a roof before moving on. And I waited.

When the stairs creaked a little and a thin slice of light appeared around the doorway, I sat up, my heart thundering, my entire body aching for her. I waited as she opened the door, the lamp held high. Her hair was a soft yellow in the glow. I lifted the covers and beckoned her to me. With her body pressed up against mine, I wanted to weep, the relief was so great.

"We need to be quiet," she whispered. "The boys sleep right below us."

"Eberhardt was here then?" I asked.

She nodded against my shoulder. "Two weeks ago. Packed up the boys to go with him."

"Did he tell you that he left four of his men in Lemberg behind?"

"No. You?"

"Yes."

"Why?"

I sighed. "Isn't that the kind of man your husband is, Cecilia?"

She raised her face to me, and in the lamplight, I could see her eyes were shining. "And what kind of person are you, Fritz? You told me you were no good."

I swallowed. "I'm not. I wasn't, Cecilia."

"And now?" She was pleading with me.

"I need your forgiveness," I said. "If you can do that, I promise to be the best man I know how."

Cecilia buried her head into my chest. I wrapped my arms tight around her.

"I knew you would come back for me, Fritz. I knew it."

I lifted her face to mine and kissed her. I kissed her harder. I kissed her to make up for the years lost between us. I didn't care who heard us. If Eberhardt's boy burst in on us, I would kill him before anyone got between Cecilia and me again. If Eberhardt himself came in, he would face my wrath.

When we had exhausted ourselves, I listened to Cecilia breathe as she ran her hand over my bare chest. I was the happiest and the saddest man in the world right then. It is the unlived life that strikes and wounds the heart of a man the hardest. With Cecilia lying in my arms, I was certain that such a pain, such a wound was enough to drive a man to lose his mind. Or seek his grave long before it was his due. I had just managed to save myself.

That night, I wished it so hard, I dreamt of Eberhardt's death.

10

───

DESERTED

1916

For two years, as members of our battalion and extra soldiers from the reserves were drummed up, I held my position on Graun's Head. I counted myself lucky. Max Junior was sent off to the south, and I worried about him. He was there with Frederick, and since I was the only son left of the Hanny family nearby, I had to make extra efforts to visit my parents.

It was difficult at first, because it meant less time with Cecilia. But I had to keep up appearances or there would be questions. I made sure to go to the inn as regularly as possible. In the beginning, Jutta had anticipated that I would come to her bed, and when I did not, I sensed from her a mixture of relief and chastisement. The nights I had to spend with her at the inn, I drank. It was the only thing that took the edge off.

On one such evening, I sat with the advisors at the *Stammtisch* and was generous with the supply of wine and schnapps. Jutta scolded me, reminding me we were at war, and I ignored her. When she snatched a half-full bottle from the table, I rose out of my seat and towered over her.

"Woman," I said, "you will kindly remember that it was my

generosity that saved this inn and"—I whirled to the *Stammtisch*—"their land. Isn't that right, boys?"

There were shifty looks around the table, and it irritated me all the more. "I am the one who showed those engineers a good time. Me and Max Junior," I reminded them. "We wrote off their bill, and it's because of me you're all on dry land."

"As I recall," Jutta snapped, "you were doing most of the drinking, and Mayor Roeschen here and your brothers—I'll give credit where credit is due—were the ones who negotiated with them."

"That's a bunch of hogwash!" My tongue was thick against my mouth. "I was the one who fought the hardest. Had to pay for all that food and drink and with my tobacco money."

The men started to placate Jutta, and I knew they were not really supporting me. They were simply not eager to see Jutta and me get into another violent spat.

"None of you," I started. I steadied myself against the post. "None of you take me seriously." I stared at their expressions.

"Come on," I cried. I threw an arm around Jutta's shoulders and kissed the top of her head, wresting the bottle from her. "Be a good woman. You're making them all uncomfortable." I swung to the men, plastering a smile on my face. "Give me your glasses, boys. I'll prove I'm not as rotten as she says I am."

"I'm happy to pay," Georg said. "Jutta, you know I always do."

"Jesus-Mary!" This had gone too far. "Georg, you're family. You"—I waggled a finger before him—"never pay."

I confirmed with the others. We were all right. We were fine. Everyone was good. I sat down and reached for the stack of *Jassen* cards and started dealing them out. "Drink up, boys. And Jutta, bring us another bottle."

The following night, Jutta and I had a real fight. I might have struck out at her once or twice. What I did remember was how she swore she would never speak to the Herr Doktor again. That while I had been up at Graun's Head the last time, he had come with some "special doctors" to examine Alois. They had once more pronounced him incurable and that the best place was an institution in Innsbruck.

I argued that it very well might be. What kind of future did my boy have here? He would be raked over the coals given any opportunity. He was five now, should be attending school the following year, and with the war on, none of us could take care of him.

"Just send him temporarily, Jutta. Just until the conflict is over."

She put her hands on her hips and slammed a plate on the table. The edge chipped, and the piece flew onto the floor.

"You think I'm stupid? You keep your parents away from me, I tell you, or I will not be blamed for what happens to them."

That was the door she held open for me. The next morning, I told Jutta I was going to speak to my parents and most likely stay the night.

"I will tell them to stay away, Jutta, but you must remember, my father is an old man and still concerned about his reputation. He is ashamed."

"And you? What about the shame you carry for your son?"

When I did not answer her, she threw the first glass.

"He is the product of your sin," Jutta hissed.

"I should never have rutted about with the likes of you, Jutta." I pointed at the door behind which Alois slept. "That could never have come from me!"

I left her like that, and I was not regretful. I had something else to hold on to. I had Cecilia.

I confronted my father and demanded the Herr Doktor stay away from Jutta. I left the Schlössl, saying I had to get back to the inn, that my wife was upset and that I should be there.

As soon as I was out of sight, I took the road that led north and across the pass. I usually came to the Müller farm by cover of night to avoid raising the suspicions of Eberhardt's boys. If I made owl calls from the barn, Cecilia would wake and meet me there and sleep in the hay with me until shortly before the boys would have to be up to milk the cow.

As I walked towards Nauders, I yearned for Cecilia so much, the pain was physical. I hurried along, pausing only to let a horse and cart by. As it passed, I saw it was filled with *Standschützen*. Someone called my name, and the driver reined in the horses. I recognized some of the boys from the Nauders company, Marius amongst them. That was who had called out to me.

"What are you doing here?" he shouted from the cart.

"Going into town."

"Hop on."

I did not want to hop on. If I got in with these men, I would never make it to the Müller farm. There would be no escape. "I want to walk."

Marius swung off the cart, informed the driver he would accompany me the rest of the way.

"Where are you coming from?" I asked.

"Getting back from the Ortlers."

I stopped in my tracks. "The lieutenant too?"

"He should already be home." Marius scanned my face.

He'd lost weight, but his eyes were still deeply set and sharp. "Fritz, you aren't… Come on. You aren't messing about with his wife, are you?"

It would do no good to deny it to Marius. He saw right through me. It was the reason he did good business.

He groaned and draped an arm around my shoulder, then rubbed the top of my head, shoving off my cap. "You're an idiot, Fritz. A real idiot."

I said nothing, knowing I had no other choice but to go into town with him and soak my sorrows in another bottle with the rest of the boys.

When we reached the local inn, Marius paused at the door. "You get your orders too then?"

I shrugged and shook my head. "What orders?"

"All three companies are heading south. To the Marmolada."

I stared at him and then back down the road where we had come, the way that would lead me to the Müller farm. I glared at Marius.

"I need to get to her. Help me get to her. I can't just leave her like this."

"No, Fritz. He's there with her now. You want to get killed or what?"

Yes. I did. I wanted to die before leaving Cecilia again.

"Come on, Fritz. Let it go already." Marius dragged me into the inn, and I stopped him once more.

"Johi Thaler."

"What about him?"

"He's got my territory. I get it back, right?"

Marius smacked my shoulder. "Of course. As soon as this war is over. It'll be over soon. The Prussians and our own military are right behind us. We're going to win this, Fritz, and then everything will go back to the way it was."

Except I didn't want things to go back to the way they were. The way they were, I was married to Jutta and Cecilia was married to Müller. The way they were, Alois was my son. Elisabeth was not my daughter.

Miserable, I had my first drink, and at some point, in a haze, I looked up at the faces of my comrades and knew I could not join them. I needed to get out of these mobilization orders. I had to.

❖

When I awoke, I spit out dirt and faced a toad staring back at me and proceeded to vomit directly onto it. It struggled beneath the slimy bile, and I realized by what was leaving my gut that I needed to get food into me. When I rose onto all fours and was able to look around, I found I was in the ravine behind the privy, covered in filth. Vaguely, I recalled stumbling over to the edge and sliding down. Nearby was a creek. It took me a moment to grasp that nobody had found me, and I scanned the sky, trying to find the sun through the trees. When I did, it was clear that I had missed the assembly. Once more, my battalion had left me behind. This time I would not go searching for them.

This was the plan I'd had, wasn't it? My hand was stinging, and I lifted it close to my face, squinting to examine it. My head throbbed, and I felt nauseated again. At the sight of all the blood on my hand, I vomited once more. No. I remembered now. My plan had been to injure myself, and like everything I did in my life, I had botched up the job. I had tried to saw off my pinky finger, and now all I had were several deep cuts across my palm. I must have passed out from the pain and loss of blood, on top of the alcohol.

I took myself to the creek on all fours, drank, heaved again, and finally managed to clean myself up enough to wrap up the hand. I needed medical attention and laughed at the thought. The Herr Doktor was not an option.

Suddenly, I remembered my rifle. All I had was the knife. I scrambled about in the bush, looking everywhere. I had learned to never be without it. I stopped searching for it after a while. After all, I had no choice but to pursue my next plan: desertion.

Cecilia was the only one I could go to.

11

THE DESCENT

1916–1917

It did not take long for the authorities to begin looking for me. I was a fugitive and always on the run. Months went by. And then a year.

Afraid that I would bring Cecilia troubles, I sneaked into Switzerland, where I would be safest for the time being. Though they fortified their borders with their home armies, the Swiss were neutral in the conflict. Despite that, I knew they would not take kindly to a wanted deserter. No matter where I was, I had to be careful.

As another autumn descended on the mountains, I knew that my means of obtaining supplies, of staying warm, of staying alive at all, were running low. In a scrapped Swiss newspaper, I read we were in trouble in the war as well. Battles to the south were leading to the deaths of locals, and our eastern front—the one our *Standschützen* had to abandon to face Italy—was being brutally defeated by the Russians.

I worried about Max Junior. I wanted word. And I was lonely for him. I had less than a month before winter would make the mountains impassable. I had to make a decision: stay hidden in Switzerland the entire winter and be closed off to Cecilia and all news, or find somewhere where I had easier access to both. I decided to make one last journey across the border with the idea that my intimate knowledge of Graun's Head meant I had at least one or two caves I could hide in for the winter. And access to the inn and its goods in a pinch.

I stopped at the Müller farm to see Cecilia that night. We made love, and she shared her fear for my life.

"Fritz, what should happen after the war?" she asked. "You will never be able to show your face here again. What kind of future do you imagine for any of us?"

"You could come to Switzerland with me. You and Elisabeth."

"How, Fritz? How will we get passes to get into Switzerland?"

With enough money, I could bribe any official. I could buy my way in, buy our freedom to be together. I needed the cigarette money.

"Leave it to me, Cecilia. The three of us will all be together when this is over."

"And little Hubert?"

Her son, the one who looked exactly like Eberhardt. I sighed. "And little Hubert."

"What if we lose the war?"

I kissed the top of her head and pulled her closer to me. "We won't. It will be over soon. You'll see."

Just as Marius always said. Only it had not ended soon. Marius. Cecilia said he was writing home. He was still alive. And right there, I began fashioning a plan for smuggling cigarettes into Switzerland, wondering why I had not thought of it before. Sure, it was dangerous. The customs officials were not wont to fool around. There were plenty of smugglers who had tried to run off and had been shot dead on the run. Caught alive, they were fined an extortionate amount. Unable to pay, a smuggler faced a long prison sentence.

Marius had been a fool to keep things safe. The real risk was for his connections on the Mediterranean route. Getting the tobacco past the customs guards on the borders was the tough part. Once the tobacco was within the empire, we had little risk of running into controllers. Our little enterprise had worked pretty smoothly up to now. I yearned to have our operation back, to have money in my pocket, but also, I saw a way to make a living with Cecilia later on.

"Do you know Marius's mother well?" I asked her.

She shrugged. "Well enough for what?"

"To find out what he's writing? To ask for news?" I suspected that Marius would report on the other boys from our battalion, maybe about Max Junior, Hans Glockner, and Jonas Thaler. I also made her recite a piece of news that maybe Marius's mother would write, get Marius to understand what I was hoping to eventually do.

The next day, I stayed near the Müller farm and waited until dark for Cecilia. She did not come right away. I saw her turn off the lamps, and I expected her in the barn just after. Impatient, I went to the door, and it swung open. She stood in the dark and then stepped out, hurrying me to the barn. Only then did she face me.

"What kept you?" I asked.

"Fritz, I'm sorry." Her teeth chattered.

It was October, and the air was cold, but she was well wrapped.

"Sorry for what? Did you not meet her?"

Cecilia nodded in the darkness, and I heard her take a breath. "You were right. Marius does write about all the other boys. A few weeks ago… Oh, Fritz." Her breath hitched, and she bit her lip.

"Cecilia? What is it?"

"It's Hugo. He's been wounded. He's not doing very well."

I hugged her to me, relief washing over me. "Then we must say a prayer for him."

"Fritz." Cecilia raised her face to me. She hugged me tighter.

"That's not… Oh God!" She covered her mouth with her hands and sobbed.

I shook her. "Tell me. Now."

When she sobbed harder, I raised my hand to knock her back to her senses, but then she looked up at me.

"Max Junior…" she said into her palms.

I stepped away. "Max Junior what?"

She wrapped an arm around my waist, and her head pressed against my body, just below my rib cage. "He's been killed, Fritz. I'm so sorry."

I grabbed her arms and pulled her off. "And you tell me about Hugo first?" I cried.

"I was…I was frightened!"

I went cold. She was pushing me up against her again, her hands on my back as if to hold me up, but I felt only cold.

"I have to go to the inn."

"What? Why? You'll get caught. Don't put yourself in danger."

"Jutta does not know whether I'm alive or dead. The inn will go to her in the case of Max Junior's and my deaths. She has to know that I am still alive."

"Why? What do you want with the inn? I thought we're going to Switzerland. You cannot have both the inn and a life with me in Switzerland."

I snatched her hands in mine and squeezed hard. "Right now," I hissed, "it's all I have."

She stared at me. "All you have?"

"Until you are with me and safe, I have only the inn to count on." She had made it clear that she would not abandon Eberhardt's family in the middle of a war. I had told her to call the eldest daughter back, but Cecilia had refused. Until she committed to me, I was going to make sure the only security I had left remained in my possession.

Though we lay together in the hay that night, Cecilia in my arms, the grief and doubts gnawed at my soul. I did not sleep.

❖

It rained the next morning, and dressed in a heavy sheepskin wrap Cecilia had crudely pieced together for me, I made the long way around back into the Reschen Valley. It took me the entire day, as I knew that the patrols were thicker now and the chances of my running into someone I knew—someone who would take pity on my situation—were slim. When I spotted patrols, I was above them on the ridge to Graun's Head. My instincts had been right. These were Prussian soldiers mixed in with our local units now. There would be no mercy for a deserter if they caught me.

A light snow was falling by the time I reached the highest point. I began my descent at the top of the Karlinbach, which dropped quickly into a deep gorge as a waterfall. I paused when I saw tracks in the mud. Someone else had been here, and I scanned the boulders above me. Someone was using this route, and pretty regularly, as I found a well-enough worn path. I scrambled down along the waterfall, slipping on icy rocks, wet from the spray, and more than a few times, I had to keep myself from stopping, afraid that if I let in to the exhaustion, I would fall asleep and never awake. The fear of running into someone kept me alert enough to push on.

It was dark in the gorge when I reached a point where the Karlinbach flowed into Graun Lake. I was desperate to get out, afraid that at nightfall hypothermia would set in. My grief added to my weakness. It took all my will to stay awake and warm enough until I could afford to enter town in safety.

I approached the inn from the southern road. As I had expected, the lamps shone in the *Stube*, and when I walked to the opposite end of the house, I found them also lit in the apartments where Jutta and Alois slept.

I backed away far enough to be able to look into the room, hoping to catch a glimpse of Jutta, get myself oriented as to who was where. I could not just walk in. I kept myself hidden near the woodpile and watched. Finally, the door to the apartments opened and Jutta came in, followed by a man. I only needed another two seconds to recognize Johi Thaler. And he was holding my son in his arms, bouncing him up and down, making Alois laugh. Jutta turned up the lamp, and even from the distance I stood, I knew that I had never seen that woman more at peace. When Johi handed her Alois, he kissed the boy on top of the head, placed a hand on Jutta's upper arm, then took a seat at my table as Jutta went into Alois' room.

I clenched my fists, felt the knife in its sheaf hanging from my belt. This would not do. This would just not do.

The rain broke again, heavy this time. Tomorrow, Graun's Head would be buried in snow. I was trapped.

I glanced at the back of the house and saw that the kitchen was dark. The cellar, where we kept our preserves and meat, was just below the window where Johi sat. I could try and break into it, but I was certain he would hear me. He would come and check. Or I could go to the back door and break into the kitchen, where I would find bread and soup, probably still warm.

My stomach grumbled, and my bones ached at the thought of another cold night. I shivered, considering my options again. If I lured Johi into the cellar, I would have to fight him. At that moment, I wanted to kill him. Option two was to get something warm in me, find a spot in our stable, and stay sheltered. I had other uses for Johi. I opted for the latter.

In the kitchen, I took the whole pot of soup, half a chicken, and a loaf of bread from the pantry. I sneaked into the stables, made myself a pile in the hay, and slept like the dead. I was awake before the cock crowed, however, prepared to make my escape before anyone could find me.

❖

The *Thalerhof* was in the hamlet of Arlund just above Graun and, for anyone taking the normal route, on the way to Graun's Head. In the summers, a number of families took their livestock to the alpine meadows below the Head.

I waited above Johi's family farm, in the field where the Glockner sheep were usually put out to pasture in the spring and early autumn. As soon as I saw Johi and his parents getting to work around the *Hof*, I made my way down, making sure I caught Johi when old man Thaler was not around.

The weather had cleared, and Johi was leading a horse out into the corral behind the barn. By the sun in the sky, I figured he would be heading into the house to have his breakfast next.

"Psst! Johi!"

The horse whinnied, and he jumped. "Jesus, Fritz. Is that really you?"

From his expression, I must have looked horrifying in Cecilia's makeshift coat. And I was probably less than easy to look at with my longish hair and untrimmed beard.

"Yeah, it's me. It's really me."

He did not seem to know what to do, shifting on one leg and another. I let him squirm.

"Are you all right, Fritz? Where have you been? Jutta's—your family's—been worried about you." He paused. "You know Max Junior—"

"Is dead. That's right. But I'm not."

I heard someone moving in the barn. We both looked at the outside wall.

"Nobody's to know I'm here," I said. "You understand?"

"Where are you staying? How are you…" His eyes roved over me. "Getting on?"

"Johi, I'm here about the cigarettes. I'm not here to discuss how or how I am not doing. Who is your supplier?"

"The one you set up for Marius."

"In Borgo Sacco?"

"Yes. Except that they moved the factory and all their employees to Linz. Their factory was heavily damaged."

This explained why he was still using the old north-to-south trekking route. "When are you picking up your next supply?"

He looked astonished and then embarrassed. "In a week again. But, Fritz, how do you plan to get around on the route without getting caught?"

I sneered. "I'm not delivering them here. You're going to bring me the next supply of cigarettes, and you're going to give me the money you've made so far. Fair and square."

Johi frowned. "Fritz, I'm working for Marius. He's not going to be very—"

I moved towards him, unsheathing my knife. He stayed where he was, but I could see he was itching to run. "I'm your new boss. Or do you want Jutta to witness what I do with an adulterer?"

Johi looked stunned, and I raised the knife to just beneath his jaw.

"You will bring me the money. All of it. Right after breakfast. Or I will come in the night like a thief and cut your throat. Do we understand one another?"

His breath came in short bursts, and I pressed the point of the knife at his jugular, just before it could break the skin.

"Fritz, I don't have any money here."

"Where is it?" I pressed the knife deeper. A small red knick appeared.

Johi grew frantic. "I bring everything to Jutta. Fritz, I give it all to her. For Alois."

I lowered the knife. Insolent bastard. Who did he think he was? My heart thrashed in my chest, and I struggled to remain in control.

"You'll deliver the money to me at the Glockner hut, the one they have for the hay. There's a stone beneath the slats. Leave it there." The shepherd's hut was just up the hill behind me. "Tonight. Go and get it from her, and bring it to me."

Johi nodded, but I could see the murderous look in his eye. I did not care. I was getting what was mine, and I knew he would tell Jutta I was still alive.

A door slammed on the other side of the barn. A woman's voice—Johi's mother, most likely—called for him.

"I'm coming." Johi rubbed a fingertip on his throat. His finger came away with a small red line of blood. "Jesus, Fritz."

"I'll be waiting. And no funny business. No going to the authorities, Johi."

"Fritz, I wouldn't—"

I pointed a shaking finger at him. "Maybe not you. But Jutta would. You tell her. Tell her I'll cut your throat if anything happens."

"All right, Fritz. I will."

I looked around, and something caught inside my rib cage. I stared at the knife, then back at him. "Nothing's ever going to be the same, is it? Marius always said things would go back to the way they were, but they can't now, can they?"

Johi shook his head slowly.

I slipped my knife back into its sheaf. "How's Jonas?"

Johi stared in disbelief.

I was simply trying to get back on normal footing. "How is he?"

"He's gone, Fritz."

"What? When?"

Johi shrugged. "About three months ago."

I licked my lips. They were cracked. "I'm sorry to hear that, Johi. Hey, no grudges, all right? I'm just so...I'm devastated about my best brother. And Jutta and I, well, you understand how it is between us."

Johi nodded, but I could still see he was wary of me. I stuck out my hand. "No hard feelings, right?"

He took it but did not meet my eye. I bent down to catch his look. "Don't forget the money, right?" My hands were shaking against my thighs, and my teeth chattered. "And maybe, you know, a bottle?"

The look of pity he gave me made me turn away. I left him like that. Damned if I was going to wait in the Glockner hut though. I headed for the cave I knew and waited to see whether Jutta and Johi would send the authorities after me. But that night, when I came back to the hut, there was a bag beneath the slats next to the rocks. Food and a good sum of money, warm clothes, and a bottle of Jutta's hazelnut schnapps. Inside was a folded piece of paper. Below the name of the person in Nauders, Johi had written me a note.

She doesn't know you're here. Leave it that way.

12

THE SMUGGLER'S WAY

1918

"Halt!" The order in German, Italian, and Rhomansh. The guard was Swiss.

I raised my hands above my head and dropped the sack. I was just making my way back to the Swiss side, using the mountain stream to keep any dogs off my scent. One more run before the winter came. One more delivery to a new business partner I wanted to make in Samnaun.

"I'm yours. I'm staying right where I am," I said to the man behind me, who would have a rifle on me.

"I'm just going to turn around," I cautioned. I kept my arms raised. "I've got nothing on me."

"We'll see about that." He took three more steps and shoved my shoulder to square me off with him. The rifle point was aimed at my chest. He squatted before me to pick up the sack without taking his eyes off me. He tugged it open, but to do so, he had to prop the rifle beneath his armpit.

"Yeah," I said. "I have a few cigarettes in there. All I got left to trade for some chickens. You know how it is. We don't get paid much for military duty. We have to take what we can get."

He did not answer me but looked inside. I eyed the rifle. From my sack, he pulled out the wax-paper packet that contained exactly one hundred cigarettes.

"This looks like something." He lifted it and waved it in my face.

The rest of my stash was waiting to be picked up by my main buyer in a ravine just a kilometer away. The tobacconist in Samnaun was someone I needed to meet personally first. The packet had been meant for him.

The customs guard unwrapped it, and four or five rolled cigarettes fell into the slushy snow. I groaned, and he picked them up and sniffed them. He tossed the wettest ones over his shoulder.

"Go ahead," I said. "Have the good ones. I have matches in my breast pocket."

He eyed me suspiciously, and I grinned back amiably. He put the cigarettes—all of them—into the right pocket of his winter coat.

"Let's go," he said.

"Where to."

"To the station. We'll take care of this now."

I knew where their hut was. It was not close by. More delay. "Are you alone out here?"

He waved the rifle at me. "Move on."

"If you aren't, then we can just handle this here and now." I trudged through the wet snow. "I've got money."

"I didn't find any."

"I can tell you where it is."

He laughed.

"Maybe you have a friend at the post?" I urged. "Then one of you stays. The other one goes to fetch it."

"Move on, I said."

He was alone then. I was certain. My offer was otherwise too tempting. I kept walking.

"You're a deserter, aren't you?" he said.

"Me? No." I thought of Hugo Glockner. "Bad leg."

"Doesn't look to me like you have any problems walking."

I held my tongue, but then he called me to stop again.

"Face me. Hands up." He approached me once more and patted my gaiters. He withdrew my knife. "This seems like something too." He bounced the knife in the palm of his hand, eyeing me. "You won't need this either now that the war is over."

"What?"

He tipped his head and grinned. "Where have you been hiding?"

I had been living like a hunted animal these last eighteen months. Getting to Cecilia had become more and more difficult. More men had deserted, which meant the local authorities were making routine controls in all the areas. I was desperate to get back to her. The last time we had been together, she had been withdrawn, distanced from me, and we had fought. I was sick with worry and had every intention of finding a way back to her after Samnaun.

"Did we win?" I asked.

The guard smiled more broadly. "You have been living in a cave. No. Your side called an armistice. Over two weeks ago."

I sank to my knees. I remembered the tolling bells, had thought some dignitary had died, perhaps the emperor himself. How could I not have guessed the bells had been tolling for our defeat?

I had to get to Cecilia. I had to. It was time. She was the only reason I had been doing any of this.

The guard jutted the rifle beneath my chin. "Get up."

I rose steadily, my eyes lowered as if to show respect or fear. Defeat. It was important that he thought he had defeated me. My knife was lying on top of the sack at his left foot. Before my knees straightened, I lashed out at the rifle tip and sent it flying upwards, at the same time landing a kick in the guard's groin.

The rifle went off, and the guard buckled over. The shot echoed on the peaks around us.

I grabbed the knife, unsheathed it, and held it to his throat. "Give me the rifle."

He lifted his head, surprise and pain mixing in his eyes.

I pried the rifle loose and leaned into him. "It's just a few cigarettes. That's all. Nothing worth dying for. But follow me? And I will kill you for them."

I reached around him and pulled out the wax-paper packet of cigarettes out of his pocket, then slammed the butt of the rifle against his head. He slumped to the ground. I checked his pulse. "Sleep well."

With the sack over my shoulder, I slid down the path and into the ravine. I had to get to Cecilia. It was time.

When I dug up the supply of cigarettes from the hiding place, I looked over my shoulder. The adrenaline was seeping out of me, and I began shaking. I could not get my hands to stay steady, and I reached into my breast pocket, where not only my matches were but the last drops of spirits in my flask. I sucked it dry, packed up my things, and made my way back to Nauders.

❖

Eberhardt was back, that much I knew. His stallion was in the stable. I stroked the horse's flank in the darkness until it calmed down a little and then sank into its box. They were all in the house—the two older boys, Eberhardt, Cecilia, and the other younger children. And there I was, my second nature turned to lurking about homes at night, looking into windows, and breaking into stables and barns and cellars for shelter.

In my last visit to her, I told Cecilia that when the day came—

the day she could finally leave Eberhardt and join me—I would leave a book of matches propped on the side of the windowsill of her bedroom. That she should look for it there every night. And then come find me.

As I waited for her, my arms and legs felt like they were stuck with pins and needles. I rose and went to the barn door. I crouched in the shadows, scanning the house. It was dark inside. They had to all be in bed. The frost on the ground had hardened into thin crystals of ice. I had to wait for her. One more time.

She did not come that night. Nor the night thereafter. Eberhardt was wounded. One arm had been lobbed off at the shoulder. I watched Cecilia from a distance as she led him about the yard, as his older boys, one hobbling on a bad leg, worked at chopping wood and cleaning stables. I narrowed my eyes at the woman I had come to love more than life itself.

That night I crept to the bedroom window and found that the matchbook had been moved. I flipped it open and saw writing on the inside. Matchbook in hand, I went around the back of the house, lit one, and read her words.

Sunday. Behind the parish house.

"You clever girl." I smiled and put the matches into my pocket. Of course, I could not just whisk her away from beneath Eberhardt's nose. She was thinking of the children. How would we get Elisabeth and Hubert away from him? Sunday was a good opportunity. Enough women had to leave Mass to calm crying children. I grinned at the idea of how she would get Elisabeth or Hubert to make a fuss. Cecilia was clever. I was certain she would manage.

Sunday was wet and cold. Snow fell, and I hid in the potting shed of the parish house. Through the smudged window, I waited for Cecilia to appear and drew back when I saw Marius enter the yard, bent against the cold or from the war. I squatted at the window and watched him just over the sill. He checked the cellar of the house, then the woodpile. He was looking for me.

I opened the door of the potting shed and whistled. When he saw me, he broke into a slow, sad smile, but when he was inside and had a good look at me, it was unmasked revulsion and shock that stared back.

"For God's sake, Fritz. What has happened to you?"

Because of the cold, I had not been able to bathe, and I had lost a tooth that had caused me great pain and which I had finally pulled. My beard had not been trimmed in so long, it hung nearly to my breastbone. My hair lay in greasy streaks below my shoulders.

Seeing myself through Marius's eyes, I could guess why he was here in her stead.

"Cecilia?" I hated the uncertainty in my tone. "It's time for her to come with me. Can you tell her that?"

Marius winced. "Fritz, what kind of life can you offer her and her two smallest? They're just children. They can't live..." He waved a hand in front of me from head to foot. "Not like this."

"She's not coming?"

"Fritz. She cannot come."

My insides convulsed. I was being pulled down, as if a rope had been looped about my insides and then everything was being tugged right out of me. I folded against the sensation.

Marius put a hand on my shoulder. "Are you all right?"

A howl escaped me. I covered my mouth.

"Fritz," Marius whispered. "Listen. Pull yourself together. You're a wanted man. There's a poster out at the constable's office. A Swiss border patrol, assaulted and wounded. They have a description. And it's you. It's you, isn't it?"

I stared up at him, prepared to deny it, but I could not raise myself.

Marius shook me. "Cecilia told me your plan. No money in the world is going to buy you a pass. None."

I fell back against the wall and rubbed my hands over my face. "I don't know what to do! Where am I to go?" I balled a fist and slammed it into the wall. "All of this. For her! For Cecilia!"

"Fritz, listen to me. I'm going to help you. All right?"

I could not breathe, but I nodded.

"I've got somewhere where you can clean up. Stay for the winter. All right? Listen, Fritz. You did a lot for me. You did a lot of good things for me. That contact in Borgo Sacco? It's saving the business."

I nodded to let him know I heard him, but I did not care about cigarettes. I did not care about the smuggling.

The bells on the church tower rang. Communion. I moved to the window and looked out across the parish lawn to where, at the altar, Cecilia would offer herself to the body of Christ. After all I had been through, she had forsaken me. Denied me!

Marius moved me away from the window. His face was close to mine. "Fritz, listen to me. They're closing the border between Nauders and the Reschen Valley. Tyrol is being severed at the Brenner Pass."

I stared at him, still convulsing, still fighting for breath.

"That's right. Graun. Reschen. Your family. The inn. They're all going to be on the Italian side. You hear me?"

I did.

"You and I," he said. "We're partners, right? Always have been."

I managed a deep, shaky breath. A second one. A third.

Marius gazed at me, held my look, and nodded slowly, assessing me. He must have seen something.

"I'm the only friend you've got, Fritzl." He grabbed the back of my neck and touched my forehead to his. "Me, Fritzl. Got it? Marius. Your next best brother."

THE END

AND THE BEGINNING

A GUIDE TO THE RESCHEN VALLEY

You can learn about why I wrote this series, what got me started, and even some history around the Oberer Vinschgau Valley, the valley depicted in Reschen Valley.

For historical background pieces, a list of characters in the series, maps and a glossary, visit www.inktreks.com.

Please do consider leaving a book review on Goodreads, Amazon, Bookbub, or any of your other favorite platforms and share them with social media. Your opinion *does* count.

1 | NO MAN'S LAND

A plan to flood a valley. A means to destroy a culture.

It's 1920. The end of the Great War has taken more than Katharina Thaler's beloved family; it has robbed the Austrian Tyrol of its autonomy and severed it in half. As her grandfather's last living relative, Katharina also faces becoming the first woman to own a farm in the Reschen Valley. While her countrymen fight to prevent the annexation to Italy, Katharina stumbles on a wounded Italian engineer on her mountain. Her decision to save Angelo Grimani's life thrusts both into a labyrinth of corruption, prejudice, and greed. Trapped between a new world order and the man who threatens to seize her land, Katharina must decide what to protect: love or country? *No Man's Land* is the first book in the Reschen Valley series.

2 | THE BREACH

Burying the past comes at a high price...

It's 1922 and a year after the Italian Fascists marched on Bozen.

Nationalism in the Tyrolean Reschen Valley creates enemies out of old friends and Katharina Steinhauser fiercely protects the identity of her daughter's father from both her family and her community. Meanwhile, the Fascists have wrested control from the monarchy and momentum behind the Reschen Lake reservoir increases with plans to wipe out the Reschen Valley's towns and hamlets. Katharina risks writing to Angelo Grimani, the man in charge, and begs to have the project reassessed. But Angelo is hemmed in by a force that steers him far from his dealings with the Reschen Valley and that which binds him to Katharina. It's the opportunity the Fascists have been waiting for.

3 | BOLZANO

In the process of understanding who you are, more often you discover who you are not.

1937. Northern Italy. New international conflicts loom on the horizon, and Italy must feed its war machine. Angelo Grimani has a plan to keep the Reschen Valley reservoir out of his father's hands but he needs a local front to succeed. He faces his past and seeks an alliance with Katharina Steinhauser.

Meanwhile, Annamarie Steinhauser is convinced her future lies beyond the confines of the valley. When an Italian delegation arrives to assess the reservoir, Annamarie believes she has found her ticket out…in the form of Angelo's son and a Fascist uniform.

Love, betrayal, and deception explode in the third installment of the Reschen Valley.

4 | TWO FATHERLANDS

How do you take a stand when the enemies lurk within your own home?

1938. South Tyrol. Katharina, Angelo, and Annamarie are confronted by the oppressive force created by Mussolini's and Hitler's political union. Angelo puts aside his prejudices and seeks an alliance with old enemies; Katharina fights to keep her family together as the valley is forced to choose between Italian and German nationhood, and Annamarie finds herself in the thick of a fascist regime she thought she understood. All will be forced to choose sides and none will escape betrayal.

Releases April 13, 2021! Order now!

Early readers are calling this "…gripping, taut, packed with moral dilemmas, and nail-biting twists!"

5 | THE RISING

A homecoming like no other.

June 11 1961. Explosions rock South Tyrol as pylons and electric masts are toppled by members of the South Tyrolean Freedom party's underground. Annamarie Steinhauser-Greil's documentary and reports on the flooding of the Reschen Valley some twelve years earlier are used in the defense of her brother, Manuel, who is facing a death sentence if found guilty of taking part in the terrorist act. But when Annamarie returns to the valley to prepare for her testimony, she must wrestle with what has become of the family she left behind, and the past that lies beneath the Reschen Lake reservoir.

Coming in 2022!

0 | THE SMUGGLER OF RESCHEN PASS: THE PREQUEL

Pride comes before the fall.

1900s Austrian Tyrol. Fritz Hanny, confident and optimistic, enjoys the prestige of belonging to one of the most respected families in the Reschen Valley. When he falls in love with Cecilia, a young girl in a neighboring village, he is certain he has found his purpose in life. Already on his way to making his own fortune, Fritz pursues Cecilia only to be cut down by one external force after another. Disappointment, violence, and conflict turn Fritz into a desperate man.

"Lucyk-Berger has explored the darker side of human nature in this tale, and she has done so with great skill and splendour. This story appalled, impressed, and fascinated in equal measures. It is wonderfully told and impossible to put down." - Mary Anne Yarde, Coffee Pot Book Club blogger

For a guide to this series, including historical notes, maps, glossaries and articles, visit **www.inktreks.com**.

DEAREST READER

Thank you for your interest! I wanted to write a piece—a short story—about the smugglers of Europe. I knew who and how Fritz was while writing the first book of the Reschen Valley series, but I was not entirely certain about how he had become that character.

Like a detective, I began exploring the historical facts and piecing it together with the man Fritz was as depicted in *No Man's Land*. I worked backwards. I did not yet know what he was risking himself for until I listened to a documentary about smugglers between Austria and Switzerland. In an interview, one expert described the reasons they slipped past the controllers at the borders. Amongst cigarettes, leather, cheese, and alcohol, she listed love.

Lightening struck. I knew who Fritz was. Within the next two hours, I had not only outlined the entire story—and determined it was a novella—but I had already written the first two or three chapters. Much changed from the original plan. I was still surprised along the way, and it has been delightful to not only create this story—to give Fritz his own voice—but to also do the research on this segment of history. In this second edition, I found it important to pull that thread between Fritz and Matthias tighter. It was as I was preparing to take the novella wide that I had the opportunity to expand on the darker side of Fritz's soul.

Some readers may find a discrepancy or two between Fritz's story here and that which unfolds in the first book of the Reschen Valley series through the eyes and memories of the protagonists and main characters. There were a few things I did have to adjust to make sure the intricacies worked. I make no apologies for it. As in real life, each of us creates our own interpretation of what we hold to be the truth as related to our personal and immediate histories. And memories are the least reliable historical resource. Why should the characters, who relate to Fritz in *No Man's Land*, be any different?

I hope to meet you along further Reschen Valley trails. Feel free to reach out and share your impressions, and do—please— leave a book review if you liked this novella. You would make this author exceptionally happy with that kind gesture. I appreciate your time and I appreciate that you chose *this* book to spend your time with.

Servus from western Austria,

Chrystyna Lucyk-Berger
September 2018

ABOUT THE AUTHOR

CHRYSTYNA LUCYK-BERGER is an award-winning American author. She travels for inspiration and is inspired by what she encounters. She lives in Austria in her "Grizzly Adams" mountain hut with her hero-husband, hilarious dog, and cantankerous cat.

Her Reschen Valley series, which takes readers to the interwar period of northern Italy's Tyrolean province, has been hailed as "wonderful historical fiction," and "a must read." Her World War 2 novels have garnered awards and recognition. You can find all her works on her website, Goodreads, Bookbub, Facebook, Instagram and Twitter.

Author Homepage
www.inktreks.com

Subscribe to get news from behind-the-scenes, historical backgrounds from upcoming projects and inspiring author interviews from the historical fiction genre.

Dear Reader, your reviews matter.
Please be so kind to consider sharing your impressions with other potential fans. Or if you were not thrilled with this book—if it did not broaden horizons, surprise you with new insights, or

move you—feel free to reach out and let me know how I might
do better.

Yours,
   Chrystyna

ALSO BY CHRYSTYNA LUCYK-BERGER

The Smuggler of Reschen Pass: A Reschen Valley Novella

Prequel to the series and a stand-alone psychological thriller

Reschen Valley 1: No Man's Land

A plan to flood her valley. A means to destroy their culture.

The first book in the award-winning series about a woman who fights for her homeland when an oppressive Italian government moves to eradicate her valley's Tyrolean identity and wipe it off the map.

Reschen Valley 2: The Breach

Burying the past comes at a high price.

Reschen Valley Box Set: Season 1 – 1920-1924

She wants her home. He wants control. The Fascists want both. Contains books 1 and 2 and *The Smuggler of Reschen Pass.*

Reschen Valley 3: Bolzano

On the journey to figuring out who you are, most often you discover who you are not.

Reschen Valley 4: Two Fatherlands

How do you take a stand when the enemy lurks where you thought was safest?

Reschen Valley Box Set: Season 2 – 1937-1949

Sometimes, when you're trying to determine who you are, what you discover is who you are not. Contains books 3 and 4.

Reschen Valley 5: The Rising (2024)

A homecoming like no other.

Souvenirs from Kyiv

Unforgettable stories based on the heartbreaking experiences of Ukrainian families during WW2

The Girl from the Mountains

Not all battles are fought by soldiers.

The Woman at the Gates

They took her country. But they will never take her courage.

And stay tuned for more books published by Bookouture, Hachette UK